Foreverland

A Cinderella Story

Sinmisola Ogúnyinka

This book is a work of fiction. Places, events, and situations in this story are purely fictional. Any resemblance to actual persons, living or dead is coincidental.

No part of this book may be reproduced, stored in a retrieval system, or transmitted by any means, electronic, mechanical, photocopying, recording, or otherwise, without written permission from the author.

© 2018 SINMISOLA OGÚNYINKA. All rights reserved.

This paperback edition © 2022

Cover Illustration: Baseline Creatives © 2014

Author photo: Babstudios © 2014

For Bissy. I said I was gonna give one to you. Keep your strong spirit alive, sister.

Prologue

The October sun blared in its full glory.

Nene stood from her seat and turned back into the vet shop, not stopping to look at her visitor. She'd been expecting him anyway, and he didn't mind if she was busy or not. Having been in the mid-afternoon sun, his cotton shirt stuck to his back, and sweat stains in his armpits patterned the navy-blue shirt he wore. His ruddy good looks had always attracted him to many of their peers, but he'd always looked at only one girl. Her. Nene.

Kunle Iwaneye looked every single minute his age at eighteen. His chest was at the middle stage of development but had little prospect of expanding much more. After Nene teased him about it, he'd started lifting weights, and only stopped after his mother pleaded tearfully with him. The weightlifting worsened his asthma attacks.

With Kunle's muscle-development programme coming to an abrupt halt Nene decided not to make a comment; he wasn't happy. He was juvenile in his pursuit of an adult body. He hated his slim chest and narrow thighs and thin upper arms. Most times, he wore clothes that covered them up: long sleeves, baggy trousers, even when these clothes hid his masculine beauty, which she also never made comments about. He always told her he was baffled everyone else thought he was a handsome young man. She never mentioned it.

In fact, Kunle was not happy about quite a few things in his life. Topmost was her. Nene.

She walked back into the office with a sachet.

"I got it for you from the doctor. He refused to take money from me," she said.

He rolled his eyes. "It's only one?"

"He gave me only one but he's sure it will do. All our customers commend it. And you can use it up to five times or more. There are a hundred pellets inside." She handed him the sachet and sat opposite him. "And Doctor said each one can do. Alone." She added for emphasis.

He studied the sachet for a while and looked at her. For a moment he must have thought of something because she noticed a change of his facial expression.

She frowned. "What?"

"Nothing."

She shrugged. "Are you coming to church with me today?"

"No," he snapped. She swallowed, and he bobbed his head the way he did when he felt sorry for something he did. "I'm sorry. Mum is home tonight. Tomorrow, definitely," he said.

"Okay."

She pouted. He stared at her lips, the way he always did. He'd told her Nse Ikpe his favourite Nollywood actress would be jealous of her perfectly shaped lips.

"Everything about you is perfect, Nene." He reached out to touch her. For some reason, she let him. "Your skin so smooth to a shine and soft to the touch."

He studied her and she was comfortable with it. They usually had these moments when neither spoke a word. Some other girl would complain under his scrutiny but not her.

"Let's go out somewhere tonight. Have dinner. Sex," he said suddenly in a harsh whisper.

His words took her back.

"No way." She shook her head. "You've asked so many times for this dinner and going out and you know my answer, always. What with the sex?" She smiled. "Is that a new line?"

He rolled his eyes, so characteristic of him, and did not reciprocate the smile. "So, you mean I'll die without kissing you."

Chapter 1

The ding-dong of the Ikoyi Ben reminded Nene of her commitment to the word of God.

She slid off her desk and sneaked into the small store that harboured all the stock of the company. She read a few verses of her daily chapters quickly. Somehow, this ritual had come to be respected by her boss and colleagues. Truth be told, they didn't know what she sneaked off to do at every turn of the hour. Like so many other conclusions drawn about her, she had never tried to correct whatever impression they had of this strange behaviour. But she enjoyed the five minutes she took out for herself when Ikoyi Ben rang. Every hour of the working day, she stole five minutes of her employer's time to read the scriptures. And she luckily had the huge clock at the town square to remind her.

Nene walked back to her desk to see the visitor walk in. She froze in time, her gaze fixed on the man, a striking figure whose confident carriage stole her breath as much as who he was. Seyi Iwaneye, Kunle's brother. It had been so long ago since she saw him last. But she could never forget that face, or the body. He was tall, always had been. Sixteen years is it? Yet his image remained stuck in her memory. Somehow, she'd never thought she would see him again.

The first time had been when he followed his mother to the workshop to choose a coffin for his grandmother. He'd stood there, oblivious of her. She'd had her first crush on any other human being. Of course, she was just eleven and too insignificant to be noticed by him. He'd been so tall then, she'd had to crane her neck to look at him. Now she just tilted a little. Because she was tall too. Nearly as tall as he was.

He hadn't changed much in all those years. Or maybe he had. Maybe her girl-eyes of those many years ago made her feel small and insignificant, as she rightly was then. He'd repeated the trips to the workshop several times without his mother until the coffin was finished. And then had disappeared from her life until now. But the fantasy remained.

Seyi didn't think a creature like her existed. Not somewhere here, anyway. She was tall, so tall for a lady, and pretty. Her long smooth legs jumped at him from beneath an ugly frock when she walked in from somewhere behind him. When he casually entered his old schoolmate's office a minute earlier, he didn't know what to expect, but not an empty office with old furniture and definitely not this ancient beauty. She made him think of an Ethiopian goddess.

The fact that her appearance was so plain and ugly somehow magnified the beauty she must desperately try to hide.

That was the only way he could justify the brown floral dress with high round neck and long sleeves. The dress would have hung on her all the way to just below her knee had it not been for the thin shiny belt she used on her waist to hold it. A dress never looked so shapeless.

Her lips. Seyi glared at them when he looked up from her legs. They were a perfect heart shape. She had lovely eyes too and her face was so smooth, almost porcelain. Her hair was all natural and she packed it high up on her head with a dirty brown ruffle made from wool. He was almost sure she made it herself.

Her lips parted at the sight of him and his throat went dry. Who was this girl?

He was the first to move. And speak. "I'm looking for Sly, huh, Pade Ojo," he said and took a step into the small office, reducing available breathing space.

She stammered. "He's not here."

"Not here?"

"I mean, he went out." She licked her lips and he looked away. No jewellery, no make-up and he was panting like... This was ridiculous.

"He should be back very—soon," she said.

Her soft, breathy voice reminded him of jazz music. A lullaby in this voice could make a man sleep forever.

For fear of staring, he looked round the old office. "I see. Does he have a number I can reach him on?"

He knew this office long ago. Pade Ojo, or Sly as they called him, brought his friends over in those days when his father used it for his law practice. But the old man died and must have willed the building to his first son, Sly. The story building incredibly stood out around the modern-looking Ikoyi square. Probably Barrister Ojo had not lost it because he was a lawyer. The town lawyer. Everyone took their cases to him. Other old buildings had been demolished by an arrogant and ambitious local government chairman.

At the time, the Ojos stayed upstairs but it didn't look so obvious Pade would live here, in the centre of town in this day and age. There was a lot of activity here now, with the shopping mall just across the road, and the improvised Big Ben called Ikoyi Ben at the square beside the mall, though it didn't look like anything was flourishing as well as expected. About twenty years earlier, some development had hit town when the ambitious leader who'd lived most of his life in the UK, brought the Ikoyi Ben and created the square.

Miss Pretty opened a drawer at her desk and fished for a rumpled business card that probably had been designed in the office. The last time Seyi saw anything like it was probably over ten years ago when he just left home to school in Lagos, and later the African Leadership Academy in South Africa. She extended it to him and for a moment he glared at the slim hand. The nails were a soft pink and white beyond her glossy dark skin. They looked well-manicured, but he could almost swear this lady had never been to the salon and may have never heard the word 'manicure.'

She looked up at him when he hesitated, and he took the card from her hand. Their fingers brushed and he nearly cursed. Did she want to electrocute him or what? And he wondered what the matter was with him. In his life, he did not lack women. He swatted them off, the best-looking of them too. But he hadn't seen anything so fresh. So skin-deep, naturally beautiful.

"I'll call him, thanks," he said quickly and turned to leave.

Seyi did not breathe until he was out in the Ikoyi sun. And it was a blaring one too. Why had no one ever talked about her to him? Well, who would have? His mother for one! She'd carried on about him marrying a city girl that would prevent him from ever coming back home. She'd even sent ladies to him in Lagos to deliver subtle messages.

"Mama sent plantain to you."

"I was coming for a job interview and Mama sent this note to you."

They were many, all local beauties who called his mother, Mama like she was one old hag. Why not this one? Could she be new in town? He thought of asking Pade about it. It would be a good idea to know more about his secretary. If he knew Pade well, his friend would have made a pass at her. But what with the dreary outfit? Maybe she was new in Ikoyi. He longed to know her. Know everything about her. Wow, who would have thought this would happen to him here in Ikoyi? He thought he'd seen them all. Then he laughed at himself as he climbed into his show-branded two-cabin, black Ford Truck. A Cinderella in the chimney he thought. He would bring her out. He knew he would. She would be a queen when all dressed up. His queen.

Seyi was laughing and thinking about her all the way back to the house. He apparently forgot to call Pade even after he arrived at the site of the quarry where he planned to shoot his documentary on the gold mines at Ilesa and its environs. Originally an electronics engineer, who'd gone ahead to specialise in sound, he had ended up being a television personality by error while working in the sound lab at a multi-national network station. The moderator of a programme did not show up. About to go live in a few minutes he spoke into the presenter's microphone when the producer of the programme called him to do a voice test. He ended up moderating the programme, oh so reluctantly.

But the calls that came in after the show beat an all-time record. Seyi could never really understand why he'd signed a contract to, first co-host a show and later anchor one all by himself. But he now did little of sound engineering and almost none of electronics. He was so into talk and had been for over five years. And he was the highest paid TV host in the country as of date. And he enjoyed what he did.

Over the years, he carved out his own show and TV stations bought the programme from him. His show documented historical, cultural and expedition sites. It was a show that had taken him all over the world in the last three years. Somehow, he had never found out why the absentee moderator did not show up at the very first show that channelled the course of his life.

He looked at the site, which though now deserted, would be his office for the next few weeks. He usually did this when he arrived at any location. He would naturally want to feel the place. He had thought Pade would provide him with some of the facts he needed but it was still alright. Besides, he'd wanted to see his old friend again. So far, the only one around.

Seyi stayed at the gold mining site until late in the evening, gathering his thoughts and communicating with the environment. More than half of the time, thinking about Pade's secretary.

Nene stood numb, staring at the door long after he was gone. She never knew him and Pade were friends. But then, how would she have known. Pade had never mentioned his name. She was sweating on her palms as she slowly sat down behind her desk. Did he know her? She thought not. But did he know about her? That was most likely. Definitely.

Chapter 2

I t had been ten years since he entered the house last but still, the memories were overwhelming.

He heard the sounds and voices of himself and his brother, bickering most of the time, as he made the difficult procession to their old room, which became Kunle's after he left home. The rambling bungalow he grew up in sat as he'd always remembered it in the heart of town on an acre of land. Most of the backyard accommodated a variety of fruit trees, the perfection of a country home. The five-bedroom house had one kitchen and a large sitting room. Two bedrooms were en-suite, his and his father's though his had originally been the guest room. A bathroom served the rest of the house.

Kunle though five years younger, always seemed to disagree with him about everything. They were two opposites. His little brother was more outspoken, less responsible, more defiant. The years apart in age made no difference to Seyi's ability to control or confront him. When they'd gone to the same school, Kunle hated being identified as his brother's brother and so be it. But despite their glaring differences, Seyi loved Kunle with all his heart and he believed his brother felt the same. He hated the fact that they never hit it off before his death. This singular event continued to haunt him all these years.

Seyi knew Kunle had always envied his physique, always complaining about his thin arms and legs and then going to weightlifting sessions before his asthma got the better of him. Well, he'd never done any weightlifting and he wasn't much of an outdoor person. In fact, all his life, he'd loved being holed up in his room fixing electronics until he discovered his new talent in talk. On the contrary, Kunle wanted to be a sportsman but the lifestyle had been too rigorous for his health. So, he settled for health sciences. He'd only just gained admission into a private university to study medicine when he met with his untimely death. Which Seyi could never disclose was suicide. At the time he'd been away for his youth service and had not had the courage initially, or time, to come home.

Standing in Kunle's room felt strange. The room looked much like his brother might have left it ten years ago. Kunle had been finicky about his environment. In that also, the brothers had been different. It was the first of many reasons why Kunle moved out of their room to the guest room till he left home. They had very few guests anyway, and whenever the situation demanded it, their mother moved into their father's room; which she didn't like much. But it trailed the stress of having either of the boys move in with the another.

Seyi did not hear his mother walk in until she spoke.

"Somehow I knew you'd be here," she said softly behind him.

"I needed to feel him. I hoped I would," he whispered in response.

He turned to look at her, and there were tears in her eyes. Kunle had been her favourite son. Another reason for the boys to be so anti one another. Kunle desperately wanted their father's approval. He hated that he looked so much like their mother; which anyone seeing him would think was a plus because their mother was a beautiful woman. But Kunle complained about his beautiful face, especially because he had men making advances at him. And their father had never made things easy for the boy. He called him a "woman-wrapper" and complained he was weak, like a woman. Suffice to say, their parents didn't have a great relationship.

The fact that their mother cuddled him only compounded issues. Kunle desperately wanted to be a man's man, like Seyi. Not a mummy's boy. Seyi remembered their father's regret vividly after the tragedy. Chief Iwaneye had gruffly blamed himself for the tragedy.

"I did not touch anything. The room is just as he left it." Mrs. Carol Iwaneye sighed. "Of course, I change the sheets every once in a while, and I clean up, but his clothes are all there."

"I'm so sorry, Mum."

Seyi pulled his mother into his arms and cried for the first time over his brother. They had not been a perfect or happy family, but they would have been better off without this tragedy. The two wept for a few seconds and then pulled apart.

His mother sniffed. "You should have been here. Your father took it so badly."

"You said you found him." Seyi arched an eyebrow. "Tell me what happened."

When the tragedy happened, it had been difficult for Seyi to come home. He was at the orientation camp and the camp commandant refused him a pass. Kunle had been buried the same day he was discovered so there had been no need, anyway. But Seyi felt bad and guilty. At such a time, families stuck together. But he had dreaded facing his parents. Or this home.

Over the years, the details about those first hours of disappointment waned. After all, he was their only child now. But he'd refused to come home always having different excuses. Now he had pushed to do the job that brought him back. He thought he'd healed enough. Besides, he felt he had finally met a woman he would love to bring to his parents and had seen this assignment as a forerunner's duty. Obviously, the issue of Kunle's death needed to be faced by their small family.

"He didn't get up on time. But I wasn't so worried since he'd been oversleeping for about a week before then. At about ten I went to check on him. His bed sheet was twisted around him in a strangled way. I tapped him, he didn't answer." She choked. "There was a strange stench."

"The smell of death," Seyi murmured.

"He was naked." She swallowed. "I screamed and your father ran in. We called for a doctor. Though we knew he was dead. We were so confused. We took him to the teaching hospital in Ife. And asked for an autopsy. He had poisoned himself."

"What did he take?"

"We didn't know at first. There was an empty sachet of something that looked like coffee beans in his waste bin but the name on the sachet was in Chinese so no one cared of course. Well, we were not sure. The autopsy report said there was some rat poison or so." She sobbed. "He took rat poison."

Chief called from the passage leading to Kunle's room. "What's taking so long?"

"We're here," Carol replied and the elderly man came in to join them.

Chief Iwaneye, a chief in the king's cabinet, tall well-built man in his sixties, strolled into the room. Seyi admired how his father continued to maintain his stature. He would look like this at the same age.

"I never come here," his father mumbled.

Carol shifted farther away from him, and Seyi wondered for the umpteenth time, why they continued to stay together. The frail-looking, thin Carol detested her husband, and the feeling was mutual.

"Seyi wanted to know what happened," Carol muttered. "It's been ten years and we've never talked about it."

"When Kunle finally reached home after driving round the town, he met no one except the housekeeper." Chief sighed. "We had gone to visit the widow of one of the town chiefs. He called to tell us he was home and wanted to see us. He likes to make such requests, constantly looking for attention."

Seyi closed his eyes for a second. "He knew what he wanted to do."

"Hmm. We were both tired when we got home and went to bed without checking on him. The following morning..." Chief shrugged. "But we can't allow this to spoil your homecoming," he said quickly pulling his son out of the dreary past.

They'd seen Seyi several times over the years, but only when they visited him in Lagos.

"Come and tell me all about your trip. And the wonderful lady you mentioned," Chief said cheerily.

Seyi stole a quick look at the room before he shut the door firmly behind him.

The family sat together in the living room and Seyi recounted his ordeals over the years and the project that brought him back home.

"Of course, I insisted on this trip because I needed to come back here." He sighed. "It was wrong of me to stay away for so long."

Carol stared at her son from beneath long lashes. She was a petite woman who had an ageless look. She was the fine one of the two parents and Kunle's fresh, pretty look was from her. At fifty-one she remained the same as she had always been though there were a few new lines on her face. Seyi took a little likeness to his mother. His strong features were completely male, but he was a handsome man despite the fact that he resembled his father a lot and he told people his mother's fineness at least rubbed off on him. Carol had never been close to him, and he neither. Like the proverbial Isaac and Rebecca family set up. Somehow, the parents split the boys between them from the very beginning; added to the fact that they'd looked for Kunle for five years before he came.

The decision to put a stop to childbearing had come as a necessity for health reasons. Carol had been advised by doctors to tie her tubes because she couldn't stand the stress of childbearing one more time.

Seyi had his father's height, towering above everyone at almost 6'3. Ten years ago, at age eighteen, Kunle had been 5'7, taller than their mother's 5'4 but not nearly as tall as Seyi or their father who were both on the starting end of 6feet. He'd hated his height along with every other thing about him. Carol had showered him with excessive love to boost his esteem. Seyi felt his mother sometimes hated him for being the one who lived.

Seyi had pondered on all of these over the years, convincing himself more and more he was right. Why not Kunle? If God had ordained their mother to be a one-child woman, why not as Kunle's mother? Part of the reason why Seyi knew she hadn't missed his coming home all those years was this. She loved her younger son. And now despised the older for several reasons, most newly because he was alive. Another reason she'd always despised him was that Kunle envied him. She knew this and had been helpless to do something about it. The anger that radiated from Kunle towards him had affected her.

Take a look at me now...Seyi thought. Could he ever win his mother's affection? All he saw in her eyes were regret, and he couldn't understand what her regrets were. He was handsome, successful, full of pride, but could she get past all the wasted years, and touch him with motherly affection? He wanted to hug her and apologise for not been close all those years, especially after Kunle died. He could see the pain in her rigid stance, the groan, and sobs that had laced her sweet voice as she spoke about his brother. There were too many regrets. Too many.

"We never miss your program on TV. In fact, we had to get someone from Osogbo to install the cable TV for us," Carol said softly.

"Thanks. You told me so last time too." He smiled at his mother. "Do you approve?"

It was more than just the question. She clasped her hand over her mouth to curb a sob. "Of course, you know I approve, I call every time just to tell you I enjoyed each episode."

Chief bit down on his jaw. "You know we approve of you, son."

Seyi felt he was being unfair to his mother, but he had to know where he stood with her. "I hope to be closer to you now. I have faced my worst nightmare so far; coming to terms with Kunle's death."

"We all blamed ourselves but at last we have to move on," Carol said. The pain and struggle she went through saying those words, evident on her face. "Tell us all about this trip." She smiled stiffly.

Seyi beamed. He liked to talk about his work. "Well, my producer wanted to capture some of the activities going on at the quarry here and the news about the gold discovered recently. I was excited about it because it meant I'll be home again. The crew is lodging at a nice hotel in Iwo. We'll work every day and move around a lot. I know there are other discoveries we'll be making."

"Why didn't your crew lodge here in Ikoyi." Carol pouted. "We have one good hotel at least."

"The only witches allowed to struggle for survival?" Chief sat forward. "So, when do we get to meet your lady?"

Seyi stole a glance at his mother, caught between shrinking back from his father's saucy comment and leaning over to hear his response. She chose the latter. They had been anxious about him settling down to a family. At thirty-three, they both had been married. Chief had hooked Carol by a family arrangement at age twenty-eight when she was a mere sixteen-year-old.

"Huh." Seyi sighed and laughed. "She should visit me if she's free. She works in a bank as a computer engineer but she's always very busy," he said.

Carol moaned. "Surely a weekend cannot be too much to visit you and also meet us?"

"Definitely. We had planned she would come. Once I settle down, I'll invite her over."

"Tell us about her," Carol said with that mother's tone he knew too well.

The two men laughed. It felt so good to laugh together again.

"Well, like I said, she's a computer engineer. She's a very intelligent, classy and beautiful woman. And I'm crazy about her." Seyi laughed.

"Where's she from?" Chief asked.

"Lagos state. She's from Epe precisely but she grew up in Lagos. Her parents have always lived and worked there. She attended schools in Lagos and the University of Lagos and then went to England to do her master's degree in software engineering. She was top of her class," he said proudly. "She's been working with the banking industry ever since and…"

"Her name?"

"Oh, sorry. Jenrola Akin-Jones. I call her Jenny."

Carol beamed. "I think I'll prefer to call her Jenrola."

"That's wonderful. What does her father do?" This came from Chief.

"He's a retired high court judge. Her mother is still serving as a magistrate court judge. She's the last of eight children. All her siblings are happily married with children."

"Wow, I now know where the real attraction came from." Chief gushed. "The large family."

Seyi nodded. "It definitely was a plus for her."

Chapter 3

Seyi didn't think about Nene until the next time he saw her.

The following day had been so crowded he hadn't the time to go after Pade. The crew set up the site built temporary structures with a tough deadline to meet. Seyi worked through his scripts and moved around the set even as the workmen laid cables, mounted stands and porter cabins needed as changing rooms. They had locals recruited for labour, and casual staff for the pre- and actual recording of the documentaries and shows. They set up on the outskirts of Araromi which was closest to the busiest of the gold mining areas.

Seyi had been particular about who his secretary would be and he'd gotten one; Iyabo, a teacher from one of the secondary schools in Araromi who was on her maternity leave.

"Where will you keep your baby while you work?" Frank, Seyi's director, asked.

"My mother is caring for her," she'd said promptly.

The baby was just two months old but Iyabo wanted the job more. To prove her point, she hung around the set until everyone closed. And got the job. Seyi did not get back home until late in the night and went to sleep immediately.

He decided to stop over at Pade's office the morning after knowing he would not have the chance once he got to set. Besides seeing his old friend again, and the woman who worked for him, he needed one or two more pieces of information for his scripts.

Pade's secretary was at her desk, tapping an old calculator. She looked up as soon as he walked in and stood.

She gave a brisk nod. "Good morning, sir."

He glared at her face for several seconds, dumb-struck. Today she wore a nylon floral dress that could drive a fashion designer mad with rage. The dress was down-right 40s style with a little more nag. There was nothing special about the way it hung off her shoulder. Still, she had an aura that went beyond what she wore. She stared back at him, as though time stood still for them. Pade broke the spell as he walked in and bellowed a greeting.

"Hey, old buddy! My God! Look at you!" Pade moved to him, clearly oblivious of the charged atmosphere, and gave him a bear hug.

Seyi dragged his eyes away from her face and hugged his friend in return. "Hey, Pade. Hi."

"This is ridiculous. When did you come to town?"

"Two days ago. I came here first to look for you." He glanced at her not sure what he expected from her and she turned away, shakily taking her seat.

"No one told me," Pade said without even an accusatory glance at the woman and ushered him into an inner office. "Come. What brings you to Ikoyi? Are you visiting your parents? On a weekday? Are you on leave?"

"Huh huh" Seyi laughed. "You haven't changed at all. You talk and talk. Where do I start from?"

"From the beginning. So good to see you, buddy. Welcome back home. Sorry, my office is a little old, you know. What will you drink? Tea? Nene!" he called all in one breath.

"No, nothing for me. I'm on a working visit actually–"

Nene walked in but was waved off. She retreated without a word.

Seyi leaned back on the hard leather chair Pade offered, hoping to slow his breathing. "We are covering events around here on my show."

"Yeah, sure. Your show." Pade smirked. "I hear you're now on NTA network also," he said flippantly.

Seyi shrugged. "I hear so too. I'm not in on the commercial aspect of the show."

Pade snapped his fingers. "Oh, but you make all the money."

"All of what I can." Pade had not changed. Still so antagonistic when he wasn't a beneficiary. Seyi leaned forward. "I needed to see you about the recording we're doing. You know, you're on ground, you know more of the historical stuff, and you can get the information for us more easily too."

Pade guffawed. "That'll cost you, brother."

"Well, why not?" Seyi laughed humourlessly. "I'm sure my producer can put you on the budget."

Pade rubbed his palms together. "What do you want to know?"

Seyi arched an eyebrow. "Oh, well, stuff. I think I'll want to see my producer about the charge though."

"Oh sure." Pade smiled. "So, how's city life in front of the screen?"

Seyi felt disappointed, though he knew Pade had always monetised everything. It sucked sometimes. Like now. All he needed was a small piece of information his father probably could give, as with several other honest people.

"Fast." He sighed. "So fast sometimes I wish I could run back home and hide." He looked around the office.

Pade followed his gaze. "Not here though."

"Nothing much has changed. Who else is still in Ikoyi?"

"Lots of us. I'm doing the greatest among the boys though." Pade squared his shoulders. "The girls, well, you know," he laughed. "Many of them just marry bigger boys."

Seyi sniffed. "You know."

Pade hissed. "Jumoke is married to the local government chairman's junior brother. The near-do-good does nothing but help his brother arrange thugs."

Seyi winked. "So, you missed her."

"She's too petty and worldly," Pade said tartly. "Our little dating ended a disaster." Seyi laughed, and Pade took a deep breath. "I married Moni."

"You don't mean it!" Seyi laughed out loud. "You hated her guts!"

"Just a roll in her father's garage, she came back with a pregnancy. What would I do?" Pade burst into laughter too. "You know her father was the DPO!"

"Messy with a policeman's daughter and rot in jail." Seyi leaned back. "I thought she was a great girl, though. I hope she'll be glad to cook dinner for me one of these days."

"She doesn't live here. She lives and works in Ilesa—"

"Huh hah hah!" Seyi hit the side of his knee. "Bad Boy!"

Then a dirty thought struck him. Why would Pade hire such a pretty girl to be his secretary when Moni didn't live with him. The smile on his face froze.

Pade shook his head. "Her father lives there now, and she wanted to be close to him." He threw up his hands in defence. "Well, she had a huge crush on you. She'll come running if I tell her you're in town."

"No way, buddy. I decline dinner." Seyi coughed. "You should join her there. On a more serious note, I think you should be living with her in Ilesa. I mean," he looked around the office again.

There was the old shelf Pade's father had lined all his law books on at the back of the ten square metre room. The old mahogany table Pade used had always been there, occupying half of the leg space. The most appalling item to Seyi was the worn-out Persian rug on the floor. In those days, Seyi had thought it was lovely. He remembered clearly the first time it was bought. Pade had boasted about it in school and they'd all rushed to his father's office to see it. Then it had been upstairs in their parlour and it had been the most beautiful thing Seyi had ever seen. Twenty-two years ago. The rug now looked every single minute its age. The curtains looked new but dreadful in its parrot colours, and excessive thickness for such a small stuffy room. Seyi thought the room had shrunk somehow, though it could have been due to the fact that he had been smaller when he last visited. Pade's father died while they were in university and the law office closed though the family continued to live upstairs.

Seyi moaned. "There's nothing you're doing in this place."

Pade sneered. "We all can't have an award-winning TV show."

"But we can have a thriving law practice in better working conditions," Seyi said.

"No way! I'm not doing much of the law practice here. Just informal soliciting. More like the Judge Judy thing off camera." Pade chuckled at his own humour. "But I'd rather be here, honest."

"You could take it on air if you wish." Seyi shrugged. "I could work something–"

"Thanks, but no thanks." Pade stood. "I'm here because it's what my dad would have wanted, and my mum was there to consider."

How rude of Pade to stand, he thought. Seyi remained seated only to annoy his old schoolmate. "Oh, how's she?"

"Dead." Pade shoved his hand in his pocket. "She died last year."

"I'm so sorry about that," Seyi said with a genuine crack in his voice. "She was a wonderful woman."

"She kept our family together." Pade shook his head. "She fell ill shortly after dad died, and I just couldn't leave her." He tsked. "Moni left."

"So sorry to hear that."

It was enough to know he would decide when he wanted to leave but his friend walked toward the door and turned when he still didn't stand.

"Sorry about your brother also," Pade said with a suspicious arch of his eyebrows.

Seyi knew he brought this up to spite him. The ever antagonistic Pade. He chose to ride on the remark. "What happened exactly? Did you see him before he did it? I still can't understand why?" He breathed hard.

This was the toughest conversation he would be having on this trip home, yet he had to have it. Somehow, he realised this was the real reason why he wanted to see Pade. He needed to talk frankly with someone who'd been around. His friend's lack of tact and taste for bullying would make him say it as it was. At the time, Pade had returned from youth corps by some deceit and was home. He'd skipped law school, deferring his admission so he could re-establish his father's law business. His mates had not understood why. Without his call-to-bar, he couldn't practice law legally.

"He came here regularly. After dad died, we thought we could use the money of a rent on this office, so we leased it to a vet doctor. A girl worked for that vet doctor, I think, Kunle was infatuated with her."

"Oh, of course, I know about that." Seyi sighed. "My mum said he was extremely melancholy about that relationship."

Pade paced now. "She turned him down continuously. Everyone believes it drove him to his death."

Seyi stood. His breath hitched in his throat. "I believe it too. God, how could she hate him so much?"

"She became an outcast of course, and still is."

Seyi gasped. "She stayed on in this town? Mum gave the impression she left."

"For a while, yes. The vet doctor moved to Ife. She left for a while around the time, but then came back." Pade chuckled. "We all made her miserable. We still do."

"Wish I would meet her. I have some hard questions to ask." Seyi growled. "Introduce us, Pade!"

Pade squinted. "Of course." He raised his voice. "Nene!" And then watched Seyi.

For a split second, the earth stopped. Surely not. Surely Pade meant for her to go get the person, the nameless person who drove Kunle to his death.

"She's my secretary."

Chapter 4

The ground shifted beneath him for what seemed like forever.

No wonder there was the "thing" he felt about her. It wasn't lust but pure hatred. Seyi stiffened as Nene walked in her full attention on her boss.

"Yes sir," she said softly.

"Do you know him?" Pade waved at him. "Kunle's brother. Kunle, your—your boyfy."

Sly wasn't a name given in school because he bore "Sylvester." Pade Ojo was a snake, the kind you hated to love. One minute he had you eating from the palm of his hand, the next choking over his poison.

Nene started to tremble.

"I didn't think–" Seyi stuttered and then stopped and looked at her. She stared at the floor, thankfully. "Why did you employ her, Sly?" He turned his anger on Pade. "Why did you call her here?"

"You asked to meet her." He winked. "And she's good. A lot better at what many secretaries can't do."

Seyi couldn't keep his hands from shaking even if he tied them. "You'll have to excuse me, Pade. I must report at the set." He dragged in a shuddering breath. "I do hope you'll visit soon and we can get to catch up on old times." He stomped out of the office brushing and nearly knocked Nene down.

The hot morning breeze touched his face before he began to breathe again. Pade had not changed and he wasn't even sure this "Nene" was the girl. What a disgusting sense of humour Sly had to employ her and make jokes about it. No one had ever mentioned she was so beautiful. But then who would have? He'd not even known Kunle had a thing for anyone. Well, the two brothers never talked. It was one of the many regrets in their relationship. Their lives had just been on parallel lanes. As kids, Daddy took him to the dilapidated Ikoyi stadium to train as a footballer, while Mummy took Kunle to the market, his brother loved it too. Sometimes he would be jealous of the roasted corn Mummy bought for her favourite boy while Daddy pushed him to be a man and ignore his mummy's-wrapper-brother.

Seyi pulled himself to face the reality of the moment. This Nene had not disputed Sly's fact, just as she had not argued the accusation of not giving Pade a message that he'd visited earlier. If she indeed was the girl who last saw his brother, then it answered a lot of his questions. She had a magnetic pull to a man's senses. He now understood why Kunle loved her and literarily killed himself over her. As he drove the truck away, he sighed, calming himself. He still had to see her, now he had to see her. If indeed she was the last to see Kunle, he needed to know his state of mind. What drove him to suicide. That would always haunt him until he knew. Knowledge would give him closure.

His mind roamed around Pade's insinuation. Nene did not fit the type of secretary described but it was either true and looks did deceive or she was one who didn't bother to defend herself. He didn't know what to believe. He couldn't shake off a strong pull towards her. A great desire to believe her above any other person, yet he didn't even know her. This was the woman he had spent the last ten years hating!

He remembered her eyes as she looked at Pade. They were empty yet deep. Beautiful eyes that showed resignation to fate. And her lips, all of her trembled when Pade confronted her. Those lips caught his attention the first time and now. It seemed to him his friend wanted to rattle her and succeeded. She must be used to her boss's mean ways unless she just resumed work with him.

Of course, she knew him from her reaction, but he could not remember ever knowing her. She must have been young when he left but would he not have noticed such a spectacular work of human art? Who was she? Over the years, all he'd heard was about a nameless girl who drove Kunle to suicide. His mother had always been too upset to mention anything more and his father posed he knew nothing about the girl nor had interest in knowing. Besides, they'd all generally avoided the issue.

For the first time in a long while, Seyi's feelings stood in the way of his job. He was distracted and edgy and by the time he got home, all he wanted to do was just go straight to bed.

That night, he dreamt about her. Nene.

It was the most erotic dream he'd ever had in his life. It woke him up in the early hours of the morning drenched and breathless. Needy. Before the sun came up, he got dressed for the day and drove to Ikoyi square, a few minutes away. He meant to be alone a little while before the town woke up, and Ikoyi square had a park of benches surrounding the once watering fountain at the shopping centre. He couldn't go to work today thinking about Nene, his brother's killer. That's what everyone called her, and he had believed it for too long. He had to clear his head.

Yet he needed to see her. There were questions to be answered. He would have to arrange a visit for when Pade wasn't there to drive him crazy. The better for him, if he got past this so he could concentrate on what brought him to Ikoyi.

Nene did not expect her morning routine to be invaded until she saw the black truck pull up at the parking lot of the square.

She sat still on one of the broken park benches at the side of the Ikoyi clock, hoping the driver would not notice her. It was tough luck; the vehicle's light was on her face. She recognized the truck as the one Seyi Iwaneye drove to Pade's and unless he had a driver who took charge of it, her nemesis was right here.

She sat facing the shopping centre, her fingers crossed, lips pressed. It was not light yet but the Ikoyi Ben had a spotlight right over it, which was the single reason she chose this spot. She could read her Bible. Over the years, someone meticulously ensured the spotlight remained in good condition unlike most of the other fixtures.

Nene lowered her head as the driver's side door opened, her open Bible in her lap, her gaze fixed on the words which now ran over themselves in a blur. He must have noticed her immediately he came within the vicinity of the square because goose bumps covered the back of her neck, and she soon heard his soft steps draw near. He came to a stop right in front of her, quiet until she looked up reluctantly at his towering figure, her heart thudding so loudly she was sure he heard it.

"I want to talk to you about my brother," he said hoarsely. She nodded. "Let us drive out of town. This place will soon get busy."

"I resume at the office seven," she said. How did he know she'd be here?

He snapped. "I will not take that long!"

Her head shot up, but he turned and began to walk back to his truck. She closed her Bible and followed him. She always woke Pade up anyway, sometimes as late as eight when she was sure she'd finished with cleaning the office and the apartment upstairs.

There was no need to make small talk in the vehicle. He drove to the outskirts of Ikoyi on the way to Ilesa and came out of the truck. She followed suit. Leaning against the bucket of his vehicle he stared as she walked up to the other side of the trunk wondering how he could want and hate a person with equal intensity.

"Tell me about your relationship with my brother," he spoke with a low steely voice.

"Kunle was my good friend. We used to talk about everything," she said quietly.

He'd not heard her say more than a few words, but this statement brought her voice ringing in his ears. There was a catch to it as though she was short of breath. He assumed it was because she was nervous. But again it was a strong, controlled voice, though husky. Her face gave nothing away.

He glared at her. "Were you in love with him?"

"No. He believed he was in love with me," she said bluntly, her gaze matched his.

She wasn't as timid as he thought after all.

"So, he had some kind of crush," he began to pace to ward off his growing mixed emotions. Being so close to her gave him feelings he could not lay his hand on. "And you led him on."

"I never led him on."

He threw his hands in the air. "But he killed himself for you."

"I—"

He cut in. "When last did you see him?"

"He came to see me at the vet the day before he died. He wanted to sleep with me!" she snapped. Her breathy voice cracked and deepened.

Her tone stunned him to silence for a second. "And?"

She lowered her voice. "I told him no. He was not happy about it."

Seyi crossed his arms over his chest. "How old were you?"

Kunle had never had sex with anyone before to his extremely limited knowledge about his brother but made that final request? He knew he was going to die? Why?

"Seventeen."

"Were you a virgin?"

"That I think is not your business, sir."

She turned toward the front of the truck, as though to get back in. He lunged forward and yanked her arm, swung her round to face him. She gasped.

He clenched his teeth. "Everything about you is my business." Furious about his lack of control and her complacent glare, he yelled. "You were the last to see my brother alive. You knew his state of mind and God knows if I prove you had anything to do with his death, I will prosecute you!"

"Your mother was the last to see him alive. She knew his state of mind," she yelled back. "She should be blamed!"

Her words drove him over the edge. He raised his hand and slapped her, hard across her face with the back of his hand. She reeled and landed on the dirt ground on her backside and hands. An effort to maintain her balance a moment before she lost footing twirled her flared black skirt out of place in a way he couldn't understand. All he saw from them on was dark, smooth skin exposed from clothing riding way too close to privacy for his liking. He took a step toward her not sure of his intent, unable at the moment to control his reflexes. She scooted back, and his breathing hitched. Did she know the movement twisted the life of his guts and made him at risk of committing an act he would not be able to defend?

When he looked into her face, his apology got stuck in his throat. She'd narrowed her eyes, blinking them rapidly, and seemed to breathe through her mouth. More than express anger though he saw seduction. It was the most ridiculous conclusion to make under the circumstances. She moved farther away from him, got to her feet and darted. He didn't act fast enough and until she branched into the woods before he hurried back into the truck and gave chase. He would not be able to catch her on foot as fast as she ran.

Women didn't run away from him, he attracted them. His hand burned from the shame of hitting her, yet the emotion his body registered had nothing to do with shame. He slowed down at the spot he estimated she diverted and would have parked and entered the bush after her, but she resurfaced, probably after realizing there was no route of escape where she'd thought. After a second's surprised pause, she turned toward him and ran past the truck. He cursed before he could stop himself. Judging from her speed, his best option remained driving. He spun the truck at a crazy angle, grateful no other vehicle passed by.

She didn't stand a chance this time. He swung his vehicle off the road with the engine running, flew out of the truck a few metres away and caught her in her flight.

"Where do you think you're running to?" he shook her breathlessly.

She did not honour him with a response and he thrust her towards the truck. He expected her to struggle but she did not. Back inside he turned to face her and noticed how she wrapped her arms around her body so tight her veins stood out.

"Have you been sleeping with Pade?" he barked, surprising himself. This wasn't what he wanted to talk about. She remained numb. He shoved her. "Answer me!"

She turned to him and snarled. "No."

He could see one side of her mouth begin to swell and he swallowed hard. He had never raised his hand to a woman before. She turned her face away, but he reached out and yanked it back toward him. His fingers trembled as he held on to her chin. He chose to ignore the flashing anger he could see in her eyes.

"Why didn't you tell Pade I came to see him the first day?" The gradual raising of the tender flesh of her smooth cheeks, nose and lovely lips distracted him. "You can't talk?"

"I did," she mumbled.

"Why didn't you dispute it when he lied against you?"

"It wasn't necessary."

His fingers dropped from her chin, but she didn't look away. He touched the dark swelling his slap made on her beautiful face and swallowed again.

He searched her eyes, his voice soft. "You're the most beautiful creature I have ever seen."

She stared back. He wanted to apologise, wished he could form the words, but he was still angry at her reference to his mother. Did she know the agony they had been through as a family? How his mother had been near to a nervous breakdown, threatening suicide herself? The friction Kunle's death had caused in the family? The shame of suicide, the stigma on the family? If he wasn't so successful, maybe his parents would have had to move out of town, the chieftaincy title conferred on his father withdrawn.

"I cannot fault my brother for falling for you," he said. "You're extremely attractive despite your ugly dressing." He dropped his gaze and snickered. "Iwaneye, you must be a fool," he whispered and rubbed the back of his head.

"I want to go back to my office," she said calmly.

He returned his gaze to her. "What did you do to get the job with Pade?"

She pressed her lips so hard it became a haughty pout. "I applied," she said tartly.

"If you continue pouting at me like that, I will kiss you. Hard."

He did not want to laugh under the circumstances, but he did. His brain was cooked. He thought she had a good sense of humour. He thought he was angry with her. He didn't know what to think as he stared until the pout slowly softened and relaxed. Sweat broke out on his palms. She didn't laugh. She didn't even smile. Her face remained stoic and he shook his head in amusement. This woman had him panting like a thirsty dog and acted like she knew none of it.

"Yeah, sure you did," he said, finding it hard to breathe.

They both sat quietly in the cabin of the truck. Thoughts ran through his mind. She must hate him for slapping her and then laughing at something she didn't consider funny. He had insinuated she was a whore for nothing. He didn't even know her. He knew nothing about her.

"Where do you live?" he asked.

He almost added a nasty indication she lived with Pade but stopped himself. Pade was married anyway even if his wife lived kilometres away.

"Nowhere important."

Her lips were regally swollen now, and he couldn't stop looking at how full and beautiful they still looked. How did God shape lips like that?

"How do you get to the square so early?"

"I trek."

"Why?"

She gasped. "It's too early to get transportation."

"Then why go so early?"

Her eyes remained on him. "So I can pray?"

He snickered. "Well, why can't you pray in your house?"

Her voice pitched. "It's not–conducive," she stuttered.

He wondered where she lived, and her reluctance to talk about it. "What time do you get there?"

She squared her shoulders. "Early enough."

"Your face." Involuntarily, he reached out again. "Is swollen."

She refused to bat an eye but shifted her gaze towards the back of his head. "I need to get to work."

He wanted to protest but to what end. He had lost control of his emotions. Hitting her made him vulnerable like never before. He needed to work on that. He couldn't afford to show so much of himself to her. Without another word, he put the truck in gear and drove her back to town.

"Please drop me before the square. I don't want anybody to see me in your truck," she said.

He granted her request.

Chapter 5

Seyi got to the square at a half past five the following day and found her pacing.

Unlike the day before when she had been obviously flustered by his presence, she ignored him. He remained in the cabin of his truck, hoping she would round up her prayer and come to him but she did not. After a while, she sat down to read her Bible. He got out of the truck, rattled by her indifference, strolled right up to her, and stood in front of her as he had done the day before. She continued to behave as though he was part of the landscaping.

"Did Pade notice your face?" He spoke in a low tone to hide his fury. "When you got back?"

She didn't answer at first, and just as he was about to speak again, she looked at him. "Yes."

He hid his surprise at her hard tone. "And?"

"And nothing. He didn't ask me what happened. He only said, 'your face is swollen. I wonder which one of them did that to you'"

Seyi swallowed. "What does that mean?"

She closed her Bible. "You should ask him when you see him."

"You're angry with me." He looked anywhere but at her. "You annoyed me. You don't say things like that about a woman who has lost a grown-up son." His gaze returned to her face. "Or any son at that." She didn't even blink. He shrugged. "I've never hit a woman in my life. Goodness, I was shocked when you fell down." He shook his head. "Then your face started swelling. You have such tender skin."

"I'm sorry about what I said," she murmured.

"It's okay." He took a closer look. "Looks like the swelling's gone too." He was right.

"I mean it. I should not say anything nasty like that, really. Your mother is a nice lady." She took a deep breath. "And Kunle loved her so much."

"How close were you to my brother?" Her reference helped him find the opening he wanted to speak about Kunle.

"He liked being with me," she said softly.

"I know how he felt about you; everyone does," he said stiffly. "What I want to know is how you feel, felt about him."

Her hair must have been plaited the day before. The style ought to leave long thin locks all over her head, but even those she packed with an invisible rubber band and tucked at her nape. It troubled him how he noticed the tiniest details even to the straight lines of her scalp.

"Your brother was my friend. I really liked him. I mourn him even till today." She stared at the open Bible in her laps. "But we represent different worlds. I'm sorry but I thought he just wanted to use me."

It was a nasty thing to say about the dead, but he appreciated her honesty. "How did you two meet?"

"I've always been around, you know. One day, he walked up to me and told me he liked me. I thought he was joking, but then he would always come around me and chat and talk."

"Around you where? We belong to different worlds as you said."

Her throat worked for a moment as though she struggled to say something. "I can't remember where."

"Why are you lying? What are you hiding? Look at me." She did. "How old were you when you two met?"

"I was thirteen."

It made him understand why he'd never been aware of her. He was away in school.

"You've always been around where? Did you know me?"

"I grew up with the family of Idowu Dada, the coffin-maker," she said simply. "I know virtually everyone who's had to bury someone in this town."

"I see."

He had been to the coffin shop when his paternal grandmother died and he'd gone to get a coffin with his mother. She was right. Anyone who'd had to bury in the town bought their coffin from Dada's Coffins. The man was the only local in the trade.

"You're not Mr. Dada's daughter, are you?"

She shook her head. "No, I'm not. But he brought me up."

"Where are your parents?"

"I don't know," she said. "I'm a bastard. But then, anyone who's bothered to have a conversation with Dada knows this."

Her brutal honesty hit him square in the face like a splash of cold water. "You don't like people being close to you, do you?"

"No." She pressed her lips to the haughty pout. "No, I don't want to have any friends. Not among your high and mighty class."

"Who are your friends?"

"I don't have any."

He barked. "Where do you live?"

"I live in a shack behind Dada's workshop. No one else would have me in their compound." She gripped her Bible and stood.

Involuntarily, he took a step back though there was enough space between them. "I guess you also do not have plans to marry anyone?"

Seyi drew in a deep breathe. That wasn't a line of questioning he planned to pursue.

"No."

He found his bearing quickly. "Would you have married my brother if he had been alive?"

"No." She stepped aside. "I want to go. It's getting bright and I don't want to be seen with you."

"You said that yesterday, why? What is the big deal about being seen with me?"

"It has nothing to do with you." She walked away.

He watched her cross the road and disappear into Pade's house. She lived there. He didn't understand her, and he had to. And his brother was only one of the reasons why.

The set had already been prepared for the first round of recordings when he got there. Frank worked eighteen hours a day, crazy with his assistant, a pretty, petite Japanese woman called Asuka who was married to a Nigerian billionaire. It promised to be a busy day and Seyi prayed he would be able to concentrate.

"Early riser," Asuka said as he strode towards the crew working on the microphones, where she and Frank tested for the right pitch with the sound engineers.

"I hardly slept last night," Seyi said, bending almost in half to give her a peck on her forehead.

She winked. "Must be a woman, I am sure."

Frank arched his eyebrow. "Jenny?"

"She's fine." Seyi shrugged. "I spoke with her two days ago." He'd dreamt about Nene again but that wasn't going to be part of the set-talk today.

Asuka pushed him playfully. "Well, call her now. You'll feel better."

He thought it was a good idea. "I will. Should get me relaxed."

"Your changing room is ready. You could go in there and get some rest. We still have at least two hours before you come up," Frank said.

Seyi sighed. "Yes, buddy. I think that's a great idea."

The porter cabin prepared for him had a soft leather sofa bed and basic amenities. He called Jenny first. She was already at work. They made small talk, caught up on the events in their lives and he hung up. Then he sank into his soft bed and drowned himself in thoughts about Nene until he slept off.

Frank woke him up about three hours later. He freshened up and the stylists and make-up artists prepared him for the recording.

"Back-up ready. Camera 1, lights. Camera 2." Frank raised his hands. "Behind the scenes. 3 and 4. Standby. Take 2. Roll."

"Gold dust has always been a part of every man's dreams. Men kill to have it–"

"Cut," Frank yelled. "You didn't say that!"

"I'm sorry."

"Take 5. 2. Roll."

"Gold dust has always been a part of every man's dreams. And here in the rural communities of Ijesaland in the Osun State of Nigeria, gold forms part of the dust." Seyi smiled into the camera. "Welcome. I am Seyi Iwaneye on Reach Africa." He moved away from the spot and walked on a dusty path for a few seconds before bending to pick up part of the dust.

"Gold." He smiled into the camera again, as he allowed the dust in his hand to trickle away. "Before gold was discovered in Ilesa, the capital of Ijesaland, the area produced only 12% of Nigeria's gold. In 1942, and for the rest of the decade, Ijesaland became the major gold area, producing more than all the other parts of Nigeria put together, due to the discovery of gold in Ilesa.

"Gold mining localities in the Ilesa area is to be found in a belt roughly 4½ miles wide running roughly North to South at a distance of about 2 miles west of Ilesa and stretching southwards from Idoka to Iperindo." He walked away from the focus of the main camera and turned. "We are walking on gold, right now."

"Cut. We take it again," Frank said. "I need life on this thing, brother. Your smile is so stiff it's cracking."

Seyi moaned. "I'm fine, you know."

"Relax. Be yourself." Frank looked at the director of photography, a smallish genius of a man. "Let's go again." He turned to Seyi. "We have an interview with the paramount ruler today. We take on more people subsequently."

Seyi nodded broodingly. "Your call."

The crew worked for a few more hours, taking different shots from different angles. When Frank thought they'd had enough, he called for a lunch break.

"After lunch, we do the palace," he said and dismissed everyone.

Seyi walked briskly to his cabin but Asuka followed him.

"It's not Jenny, is it? And it's not the lack of sleep," she said pointedly when they were alone.

Seyi liked her. The forty-eight-year-old woman had mothered him from the first day they met, and he took solace in her wisdom and concern on countless occasions. He had decided not to keep his secrets from her and she in return could read him like a book.

Seyi sighed. "You know, this is my first time of being home since my brother committed suicide. It's hard. So hard for me."

"I can understand that," Asuka said.

Asuka knew pain like an old neighbour. She had married her billionaire Nigerian husband shortly after she lost her first husband and two kids in a fire outbreak back home in Tokyo. Dan Jimoh was the sole franchisor of Hianchi electronic products in Nigeria and had lodged in a hotel where Asuka worked as an administrator. He'd met her and offered her hand in marriage. Her tragedy had only happened less than two years before then.

She followed the rich man back to his country barely three months after they met, throwing caution to the wind. The marriage, however, had worked out for her. She even got blessed with a son at the age of forty-two. And she'd gone into her main passion of producing TV programs. Her husband remained her staunch supporter.

"The first time I travelled back to Tokyo, I couldn't stay." She shook her head. "I was meant to just visit my mother for a few weeks and come back to Nigeria, but I spent three days and went to Hong Kong to finish it off with my sister," she said, patting his hand.

"I met his girlfriend for the first time." Seyi heaved. "She was the last person to see him that day before he went home. She told me she still mourns him every day."

"You may need to avoid her to be able to concentrate," Asuka advised. "It's for the best," Asuka said. "When I lost my first family, I kept going back to the neighbours who had seen the fire. I kept asking them questions about it. It never helped me to heal." She squeezed his hand. "Look, like you keep peeling a drying sore, it keeps opening and spreading. It never heals."

"You're right." Seyi nodded. "I should not see her again."

Chapter 6

The visit to the Olukoyi of Ikoyi, was a huge success. The paramount ruler received and treated the team to an elaborate luncheon. The crew interviewed him, his three oldest wives, and heir apparent, a rascal-looking man in his early forties who had never done anything for himself. Seyi lit up a little as the king joked about giving each of the male crew members one of his daughters each.

"Seyi, who is our very own son, will take the first princess," the old man said heartily.

Frank made sure the event got judicious coverage from the cultural display, to the elaborate display of assorted local food. Nothing the workaholic saw went unnoticed or could ever be wasted. Seyi already saw it as part of the montage of Reach Africa, a program which focused on promoting the health and wealth of Africa.

After the program at the Olukoyi's, Frank advised everyone to return to the Royal Park Hotel in Iloko, a fast-developing rustic town several kilometres away. Seyi had opted to stay at home rather than lodge with the rest of the crew.

"The Aloko of Iloko wants to throw a party for us tomorrow night in his palace," Frank said as they gathered around their vehicles shortly after the events.

"Seems the villages around here are starved of attention," Luke, one of the camera men from Botswana joked.

"Well, this happens everywhere we go." Frank snorted. "I gave him consent. The king of Ilesa also sent word to me today that he would want to host us."

Asuka laughed. "I hope we don't party all the time away."

"That's the point." Frank glared at Seyi. "When we're on set, we need to do business. All the parties are scheduled for the end of the production." He arched an eyebrow. "We have a deadline. If we don't meet it, no parties."

His words hit Seyi like a blow to the belly, but he nodded vigorously. Frank was right. They needed all the time available. The team parted, with Asuka giving Seyi a reassuring pat. He didn't feel like going home just yet. It was just about seven in the evening though the town usually shut down from eight. The palace was situated just behind the square and as the crew took to the other vehicles, and Frank drove a Toyota Highlander out with Asuka and two of the other personnel, he drove behind them slowly. Frank led the team and headed straight out of town.

Seyi turned at the shopping centre and parked in front of Pade's house. He struggled with the urge to come down and visit her. Asuka was right about seeing her and discussing Kunle but was that the true reason he was here? He battled with his thoughts while sitting in the cabin, leaning his head on the head rest, gripping the steering wheel, his eyes closed. The rooms downstairs, which Pade used as offices were dark. There was light upstairs though. Seyi sighed. She won't be here. And if she was upstairs with Sly, then he didn't want to be here.

He slid into gear and drove home.

Nene jumped when Pade came to stand behind her at the window overlooking the square. She had been cleaning his house like she did every other day before closing from work. Even though Pade had other members of staff working for him, he insisted Nene did the house cleaning and cooking for him as part of her duties. So, after work downstairs, she went up to clean and cook. Afterwards she treated herself to a cold bath. It was an indulgence she found hard to resist.

She had just finished and was still wrapped in her towel when she stepped out on to the passage that linked all the rooms. The bathroom, like all the three rooms upstairs were on the same side of the passage, with a window on the opposite wall, which overlooked the square. The black truck caught her attention. And she succumbed to the temptation of staring. What was he doing out there? She couldn't see well because it was getting dark, but she could see his silhouette from the night lights. Was he just sitting in the truck, waiting for her to come out? How would he know she was still here? Or was he waiting for someone else? Pade? Why would he wait outside for his friend when he might as well walk in. With his head pressed back like that, he seemed to be expecting someone.

"Well, well well." Pade stood so close he pressed her against the window pane. "What is grasping your fancy so–?"

She hadn't heard him approach. He must have come from downstairs through the staircase, or the kitchen, which were just beside the bathroom; because she would have sensed movements from any of the rooms.

"Oh! I see it now!" He exclaimed. "Is he waiting for you?" He tickled her, and she stiffened, causing him to laugh.

"No." He exerted more pressure on her wet back, and she gasped. "No."

"Have you started lying?" he whispered into her ear and bit the lobe playfully. "Or are you having a crush on your dead boyfriend's brother? Spying on him?" He looked out at the truck and blew a noisy kiss close to Nene's face. "Stalking, Nene?"

"Stop it!" She cringed, and he pressed her against the window harder. "I can't breathe!" She twitched beneath him.

"You're breathless over him? What do the brothers have that I don't?" He bit hard on the soft path between her neck and shoulder. Nene yelped but didn't push back. "Oh, I get it, they are good meat for your covens!" Pade laughed. "Okay, then. But I can have a bite of you, can't I?"

He yanked the towel from her back and pushed her away from the window. She clutched to the towel in frantic defence. He swung her away into the open passage and slapped her across her face with his open hand. Twice. She screamed in pain as her two hands continued to clutch the front fold of her towel. He tore her right hand away from the tightly wound cloth. She rammed her head into the middle of his chest in self-defence and he reeled back and tilted against the wall to dodge the window.

Pade grappled and caught a handful of her hair. He yanked her head up, bringing tears of pain and surprise to her eyes. As a desperate last measure, she twisted her head and latched her teeth on to the hand still gripping her right hand. She struggled to find flesh but hit only on his bony knuckles. Still, the pain she inflicted shocked him to loosening his grip. It was enough. She snatched her hand from him and ran to the spare room she used, locking up behind her.

Panting and sobbing, she wore her dress and grabbed her slippers. She peeped through the keyhole but saw nothing. He could be anywhere in the house from the room adjacent to hers to the master bedroom on the other side of the bathroom. He could be waiting for her downstairs too. She opened the door slowly and slipped out, her heart thudding. This had never happened before. He had made several advances but none violent. When she ran out the front door, her eyes searched frantically for only one thing.

The black truck.

Chapter 7

When Seyi got home, he felt the tiredness in his bones.

It had been a long day since he left the house in time to catch up with Nene, and there had been the first day of production with its energy-draining drama, and then a reception at the palace. All he just wanted to do was get a shower and go straight to bed.

His mother was in the kitchen preparing supper when he entered. "Ha, my dear, welcome. Your father and I were just talking about you."

He gave a slight bow. "Hi, Mum."

"I know your schedule is very tight but–" she paused and turned to look into his eyes. "I was hoping we could sort Kunle's stuff and finally put this behind us," she said softly.

"Tonight?" Seyi gasped involuntarily and shook his head. "I'm sorry, Mum."

Carol shrugged. "Your father thought...I knew it would not be convenient for you."

Her soft voice broke him. "No, not at all...ahhh." He shuddered. "I'm a little tired but I will help to sort his things. It's about time too." He sighed. "Where's Dad?"

"He's watching the evening news." He headed for the parlour and she followed him. "He'll prefer not to be involved."

"That's alright," Seyi said a moment before he entered the parlour to greet his father.

"Ha, welcome." Chief Iwaneye smiled. "They're just featuring your reception at the Olukoyi's palace. On the local station."

Seyi sat beside him. "Really."

Carol clasped her hands. "Will you eat anything? Before we start?"

Seyi leaped to his feet. "No, thanks."

"Your father and I will have supper after the news, so we can do this now," she said.

"Okay, ma," Seyi said. "I'll just take a minute to unwind and join you."

"Alright dear." his mother called after him.

"Do you think he wants to do it?" Seyi heard her ask just as he exited.

Chief growled. "He's said he'll do it. If you knew–"

The rest of the answer was shut out when he closed his bedroom door. It wasn't his idea and he hated the mere thought of it, though he agreed until the room was cleared out, there could be no closure to that particular area of pain and loss. On second thoughts, maybe it was better to eat first and then face this misery, but his mum walked by to Kunle's room next door, and he changed his mind. This needed to be done now.

"I know Kunle's room inside out, Mum. I think we should start with his clothes and shoes."

He headed for the wardrobe and yanked it open. Neatly hung and folded clothes filled three shelves on one part while shirts hung on the other part. "Do you have any plans for the clothes?" He took down the hangers.

His throat was hot and choked but he had to be strong. In the secret of his heart, he was sure his mother had patiently waited for the day he would come home to do this. He couldn't fault her. This was not easy at all.

"I'll get a bag," Carol said and hurried out of the room.

When she came back almost an hour later, she seemed composed. Seyi had neatly folded all the shirts and trousers in groups on the bed and sat beside them to study materials he recovered from the wardrobe; an album, some pictures, letters, and cards. Carol had a suitcase with her and together, they folded the clothes into them.

"Initially, I thought we should send the clothes to the prison, but I don't know what use the prisoners will put them to," Carol said chattily.

Seyi nodded. Small talk will help too. "Juvenile prison maybe, but I think the only one is in Osogbo."

Carol sighed. "It won't be right to trade them for money, would it?"

"No. I don't think so." Seyi agreed. "Unless we want to donate the money."

"He has some special outfits he loved to wear. I want to keep those...as a keepsake." She unfolded one of the shirts Seyi laid on the bed. "This one especially."

"I don't think that's a good idea, Mum. We want closure," he said softly.

Carol swallowed. "This was the last one he ever wore alive. I still remember him that morning. He seemed better from the night before."

"The night before?" Seyi frowned. "You said you didn't see him the night before."

Carol bent over the full suitcase. "I know someone in our church group who will give this away to people in the village."

Seyi scowled. "Mum. What happened the night before Kunle died?"

She sat on the bed beside him. "He came home that evening very talkative." Carol dragged in a long breath. "Your father went to bed immediately we came back. I couldn't sleep because Kunle wasn't home. He told me he was just roaming the streets."

She didn't make any sense. Which night did she refer to? Seyi frowned. "After leaving the vet?"

"Yes." She pressed her lips together and reminded him of someone else who had the habit. Seyi shook the thought off. "He wanted some rat poison. But he said he didn't get any."

"Did he say what he wanted the rat poison for?"

Carol's lips trembled for a bit. "I wish I had asked. But since he said he didn't get."

"He got. He lied to you about that."

Carol nodded. "Anyway, I let him talk. As though I knew he needed to get things out. He talked about his dreams. He was high, sort of. A lot of what he said did not quite correlate. In the past, when he was in this kind of mood, your father would tell him to shut up." She sighed.

"I was glad Chief was not with us." She covered her face with both hands. "He accused your father of not allowing him to...in his words, 'manifest himself.' He said your father will never understand and you too. He said a lot of things, and I chatted with him. I thought he just wanted company." Carol shuddered.

"Then he said, I've got to go now, Mum. Promise me you'll be fine. I told him, of course, I'll be fine. You promise me you'll be fine. And he said I have no choice but to be. Then he looked very sad and turned me toward the door.

"It worried me a little, but I waived it off. But I didn't feel okay. I couldn't sleep. After about an hour, I knocked on his door. He asked me to come in. He was lying on his bed and looked drowsy. His light was on, but he had covered himself up to the neck." Carol sobbed aloud now. "Now that I remember, he was sweaty and fidgety. I asked him if he was okay and he said he was. I told him goodnight again and switched off the light.

"The light was still off when we...I found him." Carol wailed. "The pathologist fixed the time he took the poison at about the second time I checked on him. If only I had stayed. He was dying right in front of me and—"

Seyi pushed sweat from his forehead back. "We can never fully understand, Mum. Don't put this on yourself."

"I stopped asking God. I see it as my own tragedy. If only I had been more sensitive. If I had insisted he sleeps in my room or I touched him that night before switching the light off. He might have been hot or cold and I would have helped."

"We all share the blame, Mum." Seyi shook his head. "If I had been here, I may have helped."

"He talked a lot about you that night. How your father loved you and hated him. How the girls liked your physique. He even said he was glad you were not here, or Nene might have fallen for you like all the other...stupid girls."

"You don't need to remember anymore, Mum. This issue's finished tonight. We will move on from here," Seyi said.

Notorious emotions raged through his blood cells. He grew a bit uncomfortable, partly because of the conversation, and partly because of the load of journals he sat on. Journals he planned to scrutinise when his mother was gone. Kunle's.

"Go on and sleep. I'll pack everything else away," Seyi said gently.

Carol sniffed. "Are you sure?"

"Yes, Mum. Take." He handed a thick envelope to her. "Letters from friends, mostly pen pals, and then greetings and birthday cards," he said. "And some of his poems, dedicated to you."

Seyi pulled her into his arms and hugged her, and then he covered his face and sobbed softly. Carol stepped back and left him alone. He stretched out on the bed and allowed himself one more chance at an emotional breakdown. He had thought he would not weep over his brother again but the more the last few days and hours became real to him, the more he hurt.

He stood up wilfully and packed the clothes away, as emotionlessly as he could muster. When he was through, he zipped the bag close and pushed it against a side wall. Then he took the bulky material he had hidden from his mother and tucked it under the bed before carrying the suitcase out. His parents were at the table having dinner.

"Come and eat," Chief said.

"I'm fine, sir." He looked at Carol. "I put all his personal effects in a raffia bag." He told his mother. "His toothbrush, and other things."

"We should burn everything," Chief said.

Carol flinched. "I'll take care of it."

Chief swatted the air between them. "Seyi will. Burn the personal effects. His cologne expired ten years ago. So also the toothpaste and soap. It's time to get rid of all these stuff."

"I'll do it tonight," Seyi said quietly and left them.

He heard his mother's protest and his father's angry words. It had never been easy having the kind of parents he had.

Growing up, he'd thought the marriage would not last. Daddy had an empire ruled by him and totally alien to his mum. Many times, he was caught in the middle like most children in his shoes, and he'd learned to grow up fast. It puzzled him his parents still stayed together despite their turbulent relationship. His mother had made it clear she was in just for her children's sake. Though she'd also said she didn't leave because their father would not allow her to take Kunle. That had been hard. But after Kunle's death, she stayed though the relationship did not improve much.

As Seyi threw the items in the small fire he built at the back of the house, Carol walked up behind him with an album.

"I know you'll want to keep this." She watched him but made no move to hand it over. "The pictures are very interesting."

Seyi would have preferred to go back into the house but something about the way Carol leafed through the album stopped him. Maybe this gave her a good reason to stay away from his father. It was dark, and only a single security bulb provided illumination, and his mother wanted to leisurely view an album's content?

"This—was his first day at the missionary nursery and primary school. He cried blood." She smiled but it didn't reach her eyes. "I was so worried he would not cope that first week." She caressed the teary face of the chubby boy in the picture.

"I remember. He couldn't be consoled I was in the same school," Seyi said.

"You two just never got along." She stared into a distance. "I wonder why," she whispered.

Seyi shrugged, unable to give a reply. She continued through the album, leafing through and giving little comments, most of which Seyi knew about. Kunle had arranged the album in a dramatic way, with notes on each picture, the date, location, and event. The album featured him as a baby, a child, and an adult. The last page showed a picture had been removed but the comment on it left.

"I will always love you." Carol read out loud. "It must have been that girl's picture he put there. The Dada bastard," she said harshly.

Seyi frowned. "Dada bastard?"

"Everyone knows her. She was everywhere in town. She worked at the market. At the vet, at the salon, the pharmacy. When Mrs. Ojo decided to run her pharmacy twenty-four hours, she was on the night shift." Carol snickered. "Which decent girl will agree to such a job? Men went to the pharmacy at night just to touch her!" She closed the album with a snap and then opened it quickly and tore Kunle's neatly written words out.

She threw it into the fire and ran inside.

Chapter 8

It was one of the roughest nights Seyi could ever remember having.

He took out Kunle's scrapbook from under his pillow with the picture he'd taken off the last page of his album and sat on the floor glaring into space. His heart thudded in anticipation of what he might see in there; a glimpse into his brother's life and exactly what drove him to suicide? He dreaded what he envisaged he would be exposed to as well - Kunle's relationship with Nene.

Nene's picture scorched, and he dropped it. Kunle first, he thought. He remembered the thousand-page book which had been bought for Kunle on a vacation trip to Lagos. Carol had taken the boys out for shopping and Kunle had requested first, for the scrapbook. Carol bought it. When Seyi made a similar request, Carol had snapped at him it was too heavy to carry.

"Oh, God!" Seyi rubbed his eyes and dragged his hand over the book. He opened the first page as though under duress.

Today, Mum is angry again at Seyi. Jealous of my love for my brother.

Seyi closed the book and shut his eyes tight. What a depth into his brother's soul? Love? Kunle never showed him any love!

Heroes are forever! Seyi read when he opened the book again to the same page. His picture as a seventeen-year-old with his brother was pasted on the page. His eyes pooled with tears. Kunle had begged him to show off his bare chest and when he had, insisted they took pictures, so Seyi had done a sort of striptease and muscle show. He had thought it was all a play. One of the rare ones he had with his brother because many times, Kunle was aloof and moody at home. He'd never really been able to reach his little brother.

Seyi closed the scrapbook and picked Nene's picture. Her hair combed into an afro was pushed up away from her face with a folded bandana, Kunle's. She made a vintage pose with her face turned toward the sun to expose the long smooth skin of her slim neck. Her fingers clenched her long floral skirt and held it up to just above one knee to expose a long, straight leg unexpectedly ashy and Seyi breathed through his mouth. He did what he'd not thought he could ever do to her picture, or anyone's at that.

Nene leaped to her feet when the truck approached and ran through a walkway of the shopping mall. How could he have known she'd be here. Previously he arrived at a half past five and to avoid him, she came an hour earlier. It wasn't even five yet. Why did he keep coming around? She didn't have any more answers for him. She pressed her body against the wall between two shops on a narrow passage designed for maintenance. An error in the dimensions of the path left it abandoned. Nene closed her eyes and waited. He would drive away when he didn't see her.

After what seemed like a long time, she heard a deep whisper call her out. In his voice, her name sounded different, sleek and soothing, like warm pap slid through a sore throat. She pressed her lips to curb the sweetness she must not acknowledge in her chest. He moved closer to where she was and stopped. Was he searching for her? Why? Nene knew this shopping centre like the back of her hand and she would run again if she needed to. Seyi would never find her if she decided to evade him.

Ikoyi was an ancient town which had been famous for slave trading in the Stone Age. Growth at every sphere of the economy was slow until the huge village was given the status of a local government headquarters. Being a border town to the neighbouring state, there were a lot of travellers moving through all the time. The few industrious indigenes had soon cultivated their own trademarks and travellers looked forward to buying "Ikoyi Bread" and "Ikoyi Chips" along the highway which merely traversed the outskirts of the town. With a local government headquarters, a few more good jobs were created. Progress got a jolt. An ambitious local government chairman worked to transform the town with less than twenty thousand occupants to a haven of foreign civilization.

The first chairman served for two terms, which amounted to ten years. He was an indigene of Ikoyi who had been outside the country for most of his life. When he came home after twenty years in the United Kingdom to do politics, his family discouraged him, but his determination saw him through. His tenure had been good for Ikoyi as the young man had ideas of turning Ikoyi to Little London. He built a multi-purpose shopping centre at the heart of the town and leased the shops out. It was beside the shops Nene now worked as a secretary in Pade's small-scale business. Right across the road where a small round-about had been, the chairman installed the Ikoyi Ben. To his credit, the clock still worked, even almost five years after he'd completed his term.

Rumours had it he bought the clock from the same people who created the Big Ben in London. He had tried to transform the Ikoyi square to a Trafalgar Square but what a lofty dream. Efforts to bring in at least one fast food operator failed. His wife began a fast-food restaurant, which packed up as soon as they left office. It was also difficult to get roads done as the monthly subvention could only take care of salaries and sundry expenses for running the local government area. The chairman promised several times he would accomplish these projects once he became the governor of the state. But the gubernatorial race proved too tough for the 'Londoner' and he dropped out before losing his life. He'd ended up on a board at the state capital, which left many of the projects he started uncompleted.

Now Ikoyi looked half-built, like half-finished make-up abandoned on the face of an indifferent bride.

"Don't be ridiculous, Nene! Come out of hiding." Seyi bit out. "I'm not going to hit you again."

He sounded so close. Nene froze.

"I found some of Kunle's writing and his diary." He sounded like he was circling the area now. "I saw the picture you took with his bandana in your hair." His voice receded and came back again. "Look, I know you're there somewhere. I saw you run in here." He lowered his voice. "Come out."

She couldn't let him see her. She covered her face with her hands willing herself to not breathe. Silence enveloped the environment and for a minute, Nene thought he was gone, but she saw a shadow, and then he appeared on the other side of the road. He was leaving. She didn't see him again but heard the truck zoom off. She didn't have any means of knowing the time as the Ikoyi Ben had not yet rung again. It would be anywhere between five and six.

Nene closed her eyes and waited some more. This was the story of her life, running and hiding. How many times had she tucked tail and fled, yet this seemed to be the biggest flight of her life. Seyi was a danger to her, spirit, soul, and body.

She must have waited long enough because the Ikoyi Ben clocked six. Nene stepped out of hiding, and afraid of her own shadow, sped across the parking lot, and the road. Pade's door was just a few feet away when a hand yanked her off her path and hauled her in the direction toward the side of the house where the black truck was parked. Screaming had never been her first response reaction especially when she knew who her attacker was. Instead, she went into defence mode. Her hands flew to wrap around her head, and protect it from any assault, unsure of what Seyi would do to her.

"I told you I won't hit you again." He flung the passenger's door open. "Get in!"

She would not argue either. I need to get to work.

He entered the driver's side, put the truck in gear and drove off at a speed not good for any Nigerian road. She wondered why he would be angry besides the fact that she hid from him.

What else did he want?

He would have waited beside Pade's house till daylight. He wanted to see her that badly. She had questions to answer. Driving helped him to vent and after several minutes of coursing the road and hazarding dangerous potholes, he slowed down.

"What are you hiding from me?"

Her response came so fast like she was waiting for him to say something. "Nothing!"

Seyi breathed hard. "If you think you can control me the way you did my brother, then I will shock you."

With his heart thumping so hard, he realised he couldn't drive and talk to her. He wanted to see her face when he asked about the things he read in Kunle's scrapbook, the ridiculously sexy picture he found in Kunle's album, and more. She had been lying, but no further.

The road widened as they sped past the small town, and Seyi found a bushy shoulder to park on.

"Do you hear me?" He barked. "You liar."

She turned and stared at him, heaving and huffing. What could she be thinking? The rage he saw in her eyes turned him on. A force beyond his control urged him to touch her, kiss her. He fought a beast of an attraction, yet he couldn't take his eyes off her. Maybe it was a mistake after all, to continue to see this girl. Asuka was right, he should just let it go before he made a fool of himself, or worse end up committing suicide over her. He could feel Kunle's pulse because he knew now how hard it was to resist this girl.

He took a deep breath. "You and my brother were intimate. Is that not true?"

Her gaze remained steady. "It's not true."

A car sped past and its lights illuminated the inside of the truck for a second but it was enough. Seyi's jaws dropped. "What happened to your face?"

"Nothing."

"How can you lie like this?" Seyi clenched his fist. "Aren't you ashamed? You read your Bible every day and one would think you were some saint." He raised his voice. "Who hit you on your face?"

"Your friend! Pade Ojo." She snapped. "He tried to rape me. Are you happy now?" she screeched and slapped the small seat space between her legs, her frustration evident in the jerky movement. "Take me back to my place of work."

Seyi's stomach muscles tightened and a pain he never experienced before clutched his guts. "The bastard."

The look on his face made her stomach constrict. What was he thinking, looking at her like he would hit her again?

Before he said it, she had her protest in place, and if he raised his hand to her, she would run. She always ran.

"How much does he pay you?"

"Nothing. I do it for free."

The reply seemed to catch him totally off guard. "Why?" He growled. "Are you having an affair with him?"

"No!"

"Then why do you work for him? So, he can touch you around?" He spat. "Just the way you worked in his mother's pharmacy at night, so men can stroll over and spend the night!"

She gasped. "Take me back!"

"Like hell."

He put the truck in gear and made a neck-spinning turn back toward town. Dawn was fast breaking, and the streets filling up. The heat emanating from him as he sat beside her in the cabin became choking and she let out a soft sigh. But the truck sped past the square, and Pade's house, and continued on. She resisted the urge to comment. He couldn't drive forever, could he?

Seyi turned off the road on to a dirt path which they continued on for about five minutes before they reached a clearing, and cars pulling up ahead. Nene studied her surroundings. She knew the area and how far away it was from where she needed to be. Another three hours of hiking, she should be back at work. If she knew her boss, he'd pretend she wasn't late. The two young men, Wole and Taiwo, who did a lot of his leg-work when he had contracts, didn't know what happened the day before but they never asked questions. They'd assume she decided to be late for no reason. She presumed.

Seyi parked his truck beside a porter cabin, which gave Nene a better advantage to escape because of the obscured location.

"You're staying here. Where I can keep an eye on you." He bit out, got down from the truck, and strolled away.

She watched him walk toward a smallish Asian woman, and then could not see anything again. Did he really think she'd sit still until he was done here? No one had to tell her this was where he would shoot his documentary, the whole place was well-laid out. She got out of the truck and leaned by the side of it where she could hardly be seen but had a clear view of Seyi. People arrived in minutes and before she could take a deep breath, the set hummed with life. Seyi walked into the porter cabin he parked beside with two ladies, and the Asian woman Nene saw earlier, all speaking at about the same time.

A surge of excitement ran through her. She had never seen a video production before. She would hang around for some time. This may not be a terrible day after all.

Chapter 9

F rank left the strict instructions no visitors were allowed.

And Seyi worried himself sick she would get into trouble. Why did he bring her? He could have just let her go, but he couldn't have.

"We have so many requests for visits today. Frank cancelled all." Iyabo showed Asuka a list. "Two schools wanted to come for excursions."

Seyi snickered. "This is not some silly excavation expedition."

"Stay still," Miriam, the make-up artist mumbled as she dusted his face with a powder brush.

"Sorry," he mumbled.

"I can only imagine how many people want to see you, Seyi." Asuka placed a to-do list on the dresser. "Go through before you show your face." She headed for the door.

"At least one school, please." Iyabo followed Asuka. "Please speak to him."

Asuka crossed her arms. "Seyi or Frank."

"What have I to do with visitors. Not me." He'd said it before he remembered Nene. With no visitors, where would she be? He could sneak her into his cabin though, but it wasn't partitioned. Anyone would wonder who she was and why he had her in his private space.

He just had to take her back when he had a break.

Iyabo nodded. "Frank."

Asuka shrugged. "Maybe a school. 20 kids. Problem is, all the schools will then want to come and watch." She opened the door and left.

"It's my school. We'll keep it discreet." Iyabo giggled. "Let me go and make the arrangements."

Seyi rolled his eyes up so the make-up artist could finesse the line just beneath the eyelashes.

"Frank won't approve," he muttered. "And don't push it."

Deep down, he worried about the girl inside his truck. It made no sense having her there. She'd be a nuisance on the set. He had to find a way to take her back to town as discreetly as possible.

"Yes, sir." Iyabo exited.

The make-up done, Asuka returned and banged on the door. "Two minutes on your clock."

Miriam left and Seyi changed up but didn't escape a horn blast at his door. A strategy Asuka found worked all the time. No one wanted Asuka blasting her horn at them.

When Seyi stepped out, he took a quick peek at his truck. She wasn't inside. Maybe she'd gone. It was at least five kilometres from town. Surely, she would not think of trekking?

Everyone congregated in a porter cabin designed to hold briefings tagged the drawing room where Frank had the habit of walking through the day with cast and crew before it started. What he didn't mention didn't happen, and there was no mention of excursions. The weather promised to be hot and sunny, so Frank pushed Seyi's outdoor recording up so the interviews would be done indoors when the sun was too bright.

Frank clapped. "Okay, let's get on with it."

"Before gold was discovered in Ilesa, the whole of Ijesaland produced only 12% of Nigeria's gold. This very place where I stand is one of the earliest areas visited by adventurers in the Ilesa gold rush." Seyi looked at his feet briefly and then smiled into the camera. "In 1942, and for the rest of the decade, Ijesaland became a major producer of the nation's gold; producing more than all the other parts of the country put together."

"Cut! Take it again. I need a smile from your soul, not teeth." Frank barked. He kicked a camera stand and cursed. "I've been doing this stupid line for two days, maybe it's time you call it quits!"

Seyi gritted his teeth. He'd done this short paragraph four times. A noise interrupted Frank's next take. One of the security men came with a piece of paper for the director. He read the note and swore.

"I'm not taking audiences!"

Asuka took the paper from him. "We can take a break now though, give them their ten minutes of glory."

Seyi arched an eyebrow when Frank stomped off. "What is it?"

"A school is here. From the state house I believe," Asuka said.

"Huh!" Seyi snickered. "Well, let's do it."

"I'll get Frank. They want to watch an actual recording." Asuka went after her boss.

"Just what I need," Seyi muttered.

He marched to his cabin. They'd get him when they were ready. Iyabo knocked a moment later.

"Frank wants you."

"In his cabin?" Seyi checked his branded watch. It wasn't even five minutes since he got in.

Iyabo shook her head. "We're getting back on set."

"The school children?"

"Are settling down. The teachers who came with them have them seated on the ground."

"Hmm." Seyi scoffed. "Wonder how they will be quiet."

Iyabo shrugged. "Frank will just be even more angry."

They went back out where Seyi stood shocked at the sight of about a hundred kindergarten-age children, maybe not that many but all he could see was a sea of small heads, all seated on the dusty ground in neat rows. Three adults were with the group, two men, and one female, Nene. She had a packet of sweet in her hand, and though she didn't smile, she spoke to the children, whose gazes were all fixed on her. She moved with a grace Seyi couldn't understand, and while the other two teachers got distracted by the set, Nene focused her attention on the children.

"I told you they had the children under control," Iyabo said, following his gaze.

Frank stomped by. "Okay let's get this shit rolling."

Seyi willed his feet to move. The audience was a good thirty feet away, but he felt like the kids sat on his shoulders while Nene patted their backs.

"I spoke with Pa Amodu who was a budding teenager during the gold rush," Seyi said.

An old man whose front teeth were all missing smiled to make sure everyone saw the trademark. He was like half Seyi's size and bent so Seyi had to look down on him. They walked slowly toward the seated kids, and Nene swallowed several times unsure of what to do, knowing he could see her clearly. But he was so professional, concentrating on his job, which he was so good at.

So far, the recording had gone much smoother than anyone anticipated. The three teachers who came with the thirty children were preoccupied with selfies and left Nene to tend to the children. Her mother once told her she was magical with children, but how could she know? People herded their children away from her. And she'd only ever seen her mother in dreams. Was this woman even her mother, or a fairy. An angel, if she chose to believe the word of God over the fantasies she read so much of. Seyi looked refreshed and excited after the initial few minutes of chaos caused by the children's arrival. She had been on her way out, finally taking the decision to leave the set, when the bus stopped, and the children spilled out. One fell, and Nene ran to grab her out of the way before her mates trampled her. The teachers hadn't even noticed or cared about who she was and why she helped.

"Awon Oyinbo ni o wa gbe wura," Pa Amodu said into the microphone thrust in his face, his voice deep and strong, making up for his frail look.

"Pa Amodu says foreigners came to dig the gold," Seyi said. "Remember at the ripe age of eighty-four he was just eighteen when foreign investors worked as operators here."

Seyi glanced up and she caught his gaze for a second. But it was enough to send warm fluid running through her body. He continued his presentation, smiling intermittently as he conducted an interpreted interview with the old man. She had never seen a man look so different when they smiled. His face lit up, and her stomach dropped. She had better leave before she exposed her weakness for the world to know.

Nene knew the teachers didn't care if she stayed or left. They were so enthralled by the drama of the production set, taking pictures with everyone. Any responsible school would make sure four to six-year-olds were taken back home before three in the afternoon. These ones didn't care and coming from the state capital, they had two hours to drive back. It was getting dark, and it seemed the production team would soon wrap up.

She had single-handedly calmed the kids through four hours of seamless recording, and a late lunch break. She had done her bit. It was time to leave. Leave everyone, the town. Something horrible would soon happen and the blame would be on her. She'd done it before, and she would again. She didn't know why she kept coming back, anyway. Ikoyi didn't want her. With Seyi here and her growing feelings for him, something bad was bound to happen. She needed to go.

Seyi watched her walk away. The children were still seated and Frank had decided to call it a day early. They had done much more than was scheduled. Where was she going at this time of the evening? He wanted to follow her, talk.

Frank grinned at him. "I think I'll have babies come and watch you every day. They do you good."

Seyi snickered. "Like hell."

"Okay, we're good. Team! In the drawing room." Frank yelled. "Pack these babies home, somebody!" He stomped off.

The children were herded off and everyone trooped to the debriefing with Frank. Seyi felt unsure, to go find her or join his team. Within minutes, the set was clear. The fading sound of cars leaving, those belonging to contractors and visitors and strayers. Anyone of these people could give her a ride, he consoled himself. He turned to join the rest but was stopped at the sound of approaching vehicle. No one was allowed to drive all the way in here except for the crew and cast. Did someone forget something?

He swung around to see the headlights of an old model Nissan car shine on his face. He blocked it with his hand. How did this person pass security?

Pade stepped out of the car after shutting the light off. "Hey, buddy!"

"Wow, how did you get past security?"

Pade smirked. "Hi to you too. I live here, remember?"

"Well, good for you."

"I just thought I'd stop by, see what you guys are doing." Pade looked around the well-lit area. "Am I late?"

Seyi folded his arms across his chest. "Depends on what you want to see."

"You're a very big boy now, aren't you?" Pade said stiffly. "Being on cable and national TV and all."

Seyi rolled his eyes. "The price is a big one too. Every good thing has its tough nuts to crack."

Pade looked around. "You said you'd talk to your guys about the research thing."

"It wasn't necessary anymore. We got what we needed," Seyi said.

He was beginning to have a headache just talking to Pade. The guy had always had this complex attitude he was displaying now and Seyi hated it most times. *And you hit my woman, you bastard.* He gasped at his random thought.

"Think you could link me up with any of your boys? I need a job."

Seyi scoffed. "Don't you have a job?"

"Like yours?"

"We can't all do the same things," Seyi said. "Look Sly, let's hang out sometime. Huh, right now is not a good time."

"We can't, can we?" Pade straightened as though shelving a heavyweight off his back. "Why did I know you'd have this reply for me?"

"Because you know it's the truth." Seyi patted his shoulder. "See you around, buddy."

He didn't care his friend still stood there. He started walking away when Pade raised his voice into the silence of the night.

"I'll ask her to talk to you!"

Seyi froze, feeling like he had just been dealt an uppercut. Was it so obvious Nene had some influence on him? Pade's engine coughed a couple of times and then revved raising dust. Smoke spurted from the exhaust, polluting the air and screaming the car was due for service, but the driver drove as though he had a brand-new limousine. Seyi would have laughed but Pade's last statement rang in his brain.

Chapter 10

Nene had learned to walk on the side of oncoming traffic.

That way, she would never get hit. Some cars went by, followed by the school bus. Even if they saw her, they didn't stop. It didn't matter. She would not dare enter anyone's car going into Ikoyi. Her feet hurt. If she knew she was going to walk this long, she would not have worn this slipper. The strap had been torn during her struggle with Pade the previous day, and she'd nailed it to the wooden base to be able to continue using it. Now the tiny nail hurt, and she had to remove it. If her memory served her, she had about five kilometres left, then she could rest her head, and sleep. Her sleeping mat beckoned.

She sat on the stump of a tree and tried to press in the nail from another side where it could have less contact with her foot. She looked around and the headlight of a car shed light on a small stone. She sighed and grabbed it. But the car didn't drive by. In fact, it parked by her and she straightened, her heart beating fast. The road wasn't safe, and many nights when she had to make this journey in time past, she walked through the bush path off the roadside. But again, that wasn't so safe either, and it wasn't too late now, with many who worked in neighbouring towns but lived in Ikoyi heading home.

"Huh, nobody offered to take you home?" Pade wound down his window. "Since you decided to ditch me for the golden boy."

She could hardly speak out of relief. She wasn't in any serious danger. Her boss was a coward most times and would not risk be seen by the roadside harassing her.

"I came to work."

Pade arched an eyebrow. "He hired you?" Then his surprise turned to taunt. "But didn't make any provision for trans?" He burst into laughter.

Nene held his gaze. "I was at your office to work."

"I saw your ghost." He started winding the glass up. It took effort and several readjustments. "If you like don't show up tomorrow." The car's engine quenched, and after several restarts, spurted to life.

Nene watched him drive off. At least, she got the little stone. She moved the nail where she wanted it and continued walking. She refused to think about what Pade said, or how Seyi Iwaneye affected her. She was her own woman and over the years, she had built her own support system to come from within her. An inner strength no one could ever reach. Her safe zone. The physical sensations she felt today from seeing Seyi at work were an indication she needed to disappear again, though.

She could see Ikoyi Ben ahead, but her head felt light. Another kilometre and she'd make the turn that'd lead her to the place she called home. She lived alone by choice. Living with anyone would be too much of a controversy. With the pain on her foot near unbearable now, she stopped walking.

This was the last lap, but she couldn't move any further. She considered walking barefooted but there were small sharp stones on the ground. She decided to take the tiny nail out of the slipper, rest her foot a little, then push on. There wasn't anything to sit on, and she squatted. A palm-wine tapper rode by on his bicycle. Then the harsh headlights of a vehicle shone in her eyes. She looked down and shielded her face. Waited for it to pass.

Seyi had missed her, and if the bicycle had not passed by, he would not have looked that way. He waited for the palm-wine tapper to ride by and made a U-turn. His headlights were powerful, and she shielded her face. He should switch them off, but the fact that she was on the road, at this place, left him cold. He refused to believe she had walked all the way from the production set. She did not raise her head even after he turned the lights off and came out of the truck to her.

His voice was huskier than he thought it'd be. "What are you doing here?"

Her head shot up, and she straightened. He wished he could see the expression in her eyes, but it was too dark, and his lights were off.

"Going home."

"Why didn't you wait where I told you to?" He couldn't understand his anger. A moment ago, he was scared stiff for her.

"I don't belong there."

"You belong where I say." He softened his voice and touched her lip. "You were great with the kids today."

His eyes had grown accustomed to the darkness around them, and he noticed the slight slouch in her gait. Fatigue. Well, he was tired too, and wanted to go home and sleep, but now he couldn't. She didn't respond to his compliment.

"I'll take you home," he said.

"That won't be necessary."

He had turned to return to the truck, sure she would be grateful for a ride home. He swung around. "Get in. I'll take you home."

She didn't argue as he had come to realize she would not. He noticed she walked with a slight limp, and of course, how wouldn't she? The production set was at least a-fifteen-minute drive from town, and she was close already. He could imagine she'd been walking for two hours or more.

Inside the cabin, he felt even closer to her. He knew the energy he'd put in on the production today was mainly because of her, besides the fact that he felt a strange longing to impress her, it was as though they were a team. He hated to see it this way, yet he loved the way it made him feel.

He stole a glance at her. "You must be hungry."

She shook her head.

He smiled. "I know you will not accept. We're going to eat. I'm hungry."

She seemed morose, and much as he wanted to have a conversation with her, he didn't. He'd dreamt of her every day since he arrived. Some days he wanted the dream to not end.

He parked the truck at a famous joint many people in Ikoyi ate at. The restaurant served the best fried plantain and yam in the town, with fried palm oil stew and assorted meats.

Seyi got out of the truck and stared at Nene who remained in her seat, looking ahead. He got back inside.

"Do you want me to force you to come and eat?"

Nene twisted her fingers in her laps. "They won't serve me food. Here."

Her words stuck in his gut. "Why won't they?" But he knew two things; the answer to his question, and that she would not answer him.

"I'm going to buy the food and bring it here. And be ready to answer that question when I return." He came out of the truck but before closing the door, muttered, "and be here when I come back."

Nene watched him go and continued to twist her fingers. Better to leave and offend him than stay and not be able to control the consequences of being seen with him. She didn't want to cry now but she fought it hard. He was the last person she wanted to be nice to her. They'd poison him and soon, she'd be like trash to him too. She shouldn't care but she did. And this is why it hurt her more. She did not want to feel anything for him or anyone. His initial anger and hostility she could handle but not any form of tenderness.

He walked back to the truck with a bag of hot food, and a smile on his face. Her stomach sank. He looked so good but she wasn't, couldn't be the one for him. His mother would kill him rather than let her have him. And the whole of Ikoyi stood behind Carol Iwaneye. Nene had only refused to give up on herself. She could have left, she had…

He entered the truck. "We got lucky. People gave me a chance to jump the long queue." He placed the bag between them. "I've missed this woman's food." He brought out two foil plates and two plastic bottles of soft drinks. "What do you want? Coke or Fanta?"

No one ever asked what drink she wanted. "Any one is fine," she mumbled.

"You're so morose. At least I've bought dinner, and I'm taking you home now." He winked. "Okay, I'm sorry for this morning."

His playful attitude disturbed her. She swallowed because she didn't want to break down now. She could feel his gaze on her, on the tears that trickled down her cheeks. His thumb touched a drop before it touched her upper lip, and all her pent-up pain erupted.

"I'm sorry," she sobbed. "I'm sorry."

He pulled her into his arms and took a sip of her upper lip. She jerked back but he didn't let her move away. Instead, he laid her head on his chest.

"Ssh. It's okay," he cooed. "You'll be fine. Ssh."

Chapter 11

Nene could not let him take such liberties with her.

She couldn't afford to lose control in this way. She moved into her seat and took a deep breath.

Seyi drew in a ragged breath, removed a perfumed handkerchief from his pocket and gave her. "Stop crying, eat."

He opened the first plate of steaming fried plantain and yam, and then the other, which contained the fried stew and assorted meats.

"Hmm," he sighed. "When we were boys, I'd take my dad's car in the night and come here with friends. My mum always caught me, and made sure Daddy beat the living daylight out of me." He chuckled.

She didn't know what to say. Making friends with him would cause more trouble than she wanted in her life. He acted as though he didn't notice her weird silence. Maybe, he'd accepted she wasn't going to make small talk.

He took one long piece of yam and bit into it. "Nobody makes fried yam like this woman."

"They said she used, jazz," Nene blurted. "It's not true."

Seyi laughed. "Small town talk. The food is good."

She pressed her lips together. She shouldn't have said anything. It was none of her business now. She looked out of the window, and her gaze caught that of Mr. Albert, the big-time watch-doctor. He had a girl on his arm. Someone younger than his first daughter. Nene snapped her face away quickly. Albert was not good news especially when caught cheating. Not as though she had anyone to tell. It was none of her business too.

Seyi cleared his throat. "I said how do you know it's not true."

Nene shrugged. "I know. The food is good."

"And you're not eating." He picked a small piece of shaki and bit into it. "Hmm."

Her mouth watered, and she shyly took a piece of fried plantain. It had been so long since she ate this food last.

"Talk to me. How do you know the food is not jazzed?"

"I worked for her. She-" She took another piece, and another, her taste buds fired up, and hunger she thought she could control, raged.

Seyi ate leisurely. "She?"

She shrugged. "She cooks well."

"Did she pay you well?"

Nene gasped. "She fed me."

"Huh, that arrangement is not fair."

"I was fine with it." She shrugged again. "I don't need much."

He opened the bottle of Fanta and gave her. She mumbled her appreciation and gulped the drink. Her parched throat soothed.

He took a long gulp from his coke too. "So, why did you stop working for her?"

"It's a long story. I."

"I want to hear it." He leaned back. "I'm not in a hurry."

She dropped her gaze to her hands. "People are looking at us."

"Then we can take you home and talk." He cleaned his hand on the paper napkin he brought with the food and reversed the truck. "Tell me where."

She hesitated. This would not end well. "I—We can just park by the road."

He smirked. "You don't want me to know your house?"

Nene shook her head. "No."

He laughed. "Okay, by the road, then."

She wanted him to drop the subject of who she worked or did not work for. This was Ikoyi, a small town with a history. People didn't love people here, and many times, she had sacrificed herself for the sake of peace. She was the underdog. The convenient culprit. The same people who threw stones at her by day sought her help by night but she couldn't tell him all this. She directed him to Dada's house and showed him where to park the truck, partly hidden by a huge tree.

"Here, no one will see us."

"Why are you so afraid of people? What did you do?"

He asked the second question as though it was a joke, but she knew he meant it.

"People—I didn't—" She took a deep breath. Better tell one at least so he'd know who he was dealing with. "Mrs. Bello owned the restaurant. And she would come to Dada's house. She's Mrs. Dada's friend." She paused. "One day, I was working, in the...yard, and she asked Mrs. Dada to loan me to her."

"How old were you?"

She knew but took a moment as though she had to think. "Six. Or seven. I was small."

"Okay."

"I went to work at the restaurant. Since then, sometimes she will send for me. And I will work for her."

He pressed on. "You didn't tell me why you stopped working for her. You make it look like there's a story there."

"The first time I went, she told Mrs. Dada I had good luck. Her food is good, so I don't know what she was talking about." She drew in a shuddering breath. "Anytime I go to work for her, she makes good sales and favour just come to her." She squared her shoulders. "At least, she said so, once."

"So, what happened?"

"Her husband started cheating. She blamed me."

Seyi lifted her chin. "Cheating with you?"

"No. Never–" He narrowed his eyes. She dropped her gaze. "He was sleeping with her sister."

"Goodness, then why blame you?"

"I'm easier."

He gasped. "Are you kidding? How are you easier?"

These stories were better left unsaid. "I worked there, and I saw what went on days and on the nights, we closed too late."

"Oh, you snitched?"

"No. They knew I knew." She rubbed her temple. A headache fast settled in. "The first time, I was just ten years old. She took me to the market and made people throw stones at me."

Seyi cursed. "Dear Lord. What did Mrs. Dada do?"

"She joined them."

Chapter 12

S he didn't want him, or why would she jerk away from his kiss.

Seyi had an active headache when he got home, emotions erupting within him in torrents. His heart thudded from need and the cruelty Nene described. Why would anyone treat a child like that? She didn't want to say more after that, and he couldn't take more either.

"I'll pick you up here tomorrow morning," he'd said, and with that, let her go.

She didn't even have a good pair of shoes. He'd have to take one from his mum's wardrobe just for the following day, then he could find time during the day to take her shopping. Carol must not know about this. He worried about Nene's size too. His mother was quite small and unlike Nene.

He groaned. "Oh, tomorrow will take care of itself." He'd still take the shoes.

He entered the house through the back door and stopped short in the kitchen when he heard his name. His mother had a guest.

"Warn my son?"

"I think he came into town two days ago?"

Seyi moved to the kitchen door and peeped between the hinge. He recognized the visitor as Olori, the king's first wife.

Carol clasped her hands. "He–yes."

Seyi could see both women were on their feet so the Olori either just arrived or was on her way out. The two women had never been the best of friends so this must be interesting.

"Well," Olori shrugged with a superior air. "I have been seeing him for the past two or three days," she paused. Carol clenched her fists. "With no other but that harlot, the village harlot."

"Nene?" Carol exclaimed. "You saw my son with Nene?"

"Right in the early hours of the morning," Olori said with a low, conspiratorial voice. "In fact, for the past three days. Each time, they drive off together to a lonely place."

"I don't believe you," Carol blurted. "My son would never associate with such a wretch."

"Well," Olori batted her eyes. "I believe you trust your son. But when he's leaving the house by as early as five thirty tomorrow morning, you may want to ask him to where." She stomped towards the door.

Carol hurried after her and dragged her hand. "Please, Olori, forgive me. I just find it hard to believe. Not that I don't believe you but where would they have met? How?" Carol looked genuinely perplexed.

Olori folded her arms across her chest. "I wake up early and move around the house as you know, praying before my children wake up. I just saw her that morning, pacing and making her incantations as usual. You remember when I complained to Kabiyesi about her wizardry, he asked that she be brought to his palace. And we all know what he does to young women who enter his palace." Olori hissed. "Especially someone like that. Anyway, during my walk I saw her and then your son drove up and they leave together." Olori kissed her teeth. "I stood there until all the children woke but they didn't come back. I didn't want to come and tell you at first, but this morning, something different happened." Olori walked back and took a seat.

"They hugged and kissed before leaving then I knew that indeed, you had to be told." The woman clapped fat, bejewelled hands.

Carol screeched. "Where?"

"Right in front of the square! By Pade Ojo's house."

Seyi couldn't take any more. He walked in and the Olori jumped to her feet, an immediate smile sprung on her face.

Seyi greeted in the traditional prostrate manner. "Good evening, ma."

"Ah, my son, welcome. Your mother was just telling me about your work." Olori patted Seyi's back and he stood. "I have to go, Mama Seyi, so you and your son can have your privacy." She didn't wait for a response and saw herself out the door.

The moment she was gone, Seyi exploded. "Is that the kind of woman you listen to?"

Carol snapped out of her stunned derision and yelled back. "Seyi! You want to kill me? What are you doing?"

"Nothing!"

She lowered her voice. "You are my only child, Seyi. I have no other–" She swallowed and continued with great effort. "And I want the best for you." She paused. "I know you are grown up, and you know the best for you, but I am your mother. I don't want to lose you."

Seyi paced, taking calming breaths. "Mum, it's alright. Com'on, I won't disappoint you, and I won't die for God's sake."

She raised her voice. "Then stop seeing her. Stop seeing that girl!"

"Nene?" He dropped into a seat, suddenly so tired.

"That girl, Seyi please." Carol moved to sit on the stool by the side of the single sofa he occupied. She sniffed before continuing. "She has powers over men. And she uses it to destroy them. No man has gone unscathed. She's an ogbanje!" Carol whispered, as though scared to talk about it.

Seyi glared at her. "Why would you think I'm seeing her in that regard?"

"Olori saw you with her, at the square." She drew in a long breath. "Ikoyi is such a small place, dear. Everybody sees everything. The palace is right there at the square. You can't see that girl, Seyi, please. She swallows men. She's evil."

"Olori should mind her own bloody business." Seyi rubbed his temple and nodded trying to convince himself. "I understand if you don't want me to see her in public because tongues wag," he said. "But to say she's evil," he shook his head. "That, I don't understand."

"What don't you understand there?" She jumped to her feet. "She drove your brother to suicide. She sleeps with men and eats up their destinies. Is that not evil?" She wailed. "Look at your friend, Pade. He's a near-do-good. Ever since he employed that girl there has been no progress in his life." She began to pace frantically. "His marriage is finished, he has no money, he's in one trouble or the other."

"Pade has always been a fool."

Carol continued as though he hadn't spoken. "Why do you think no one agreed to employ her? Her uncle threw her out of his house, and now she lives in a shack! What more can I say, Seyi? She drove your brother to suicide." She sobbed. "See what she did to Adunola and her husband. And countless other young men in this town." Carol turned only her face to him.

"The only reason why I'm seeing her is because I want to find out why Kunle would kill himself because of her," Seyi said, but his reason sounded lame even in his own ears.

"Then why do you kiss her?" Carol shouted.

"I did not kiss her!" Seyi exclaimed. "This is so ridiculous. Whoever told you this, is lying."

For a moment, mother and son stared down one another then Carol turned fully and went to kneel beside his seat, holding his gaze.

"Just please, stop seeing her. Look, I know what I am saying. She has destroyed enough men in this town. She doesn't come on to them physically. She enters their dream and sleeps with them. They become addicted to her, and that is the beginning of the end."

Seyi gulped air through his mouth. Nene was always in his dreams.

Chief Iwaneye walked in, his face drawn. He didn't show any sign he could feel the tension in the room. Carol gasped at the slight sway to his walk.

Seyi grabbed his shoulder half-way as he sat heavily on the couch. "Daddy, are you okay?"

"The Olukoyi is dead."

Chapter 13

Nene was not under the tree the following morning when he arrived, his mother's open-toe slippers safely hidden under the driver's seat. With the news of the Olukoyi's death the night before, his father had warned him not to leave the house too early. Until a new king was installed, there would be a curfew. He wished he'd followed his instincts and come back the night before to find her, give her the news of the probable curfew but she would not have been there, anyway. And he wasn't sure who to ask where to find her. The people of Ikoyi had no good use for Nene and would not help him, he concluded. He still needed to get to the truth of this matter. Nene had still not told him why she was so hated, even as a child. And he had some more questions about Kunle's death.

He'd sent a message to Frank about the new curfew and told him to keep it silent. There would no longer be visits on the set, for security reasons.

"We're rounding off this production tomorrow. I'm not ready to follow your king to the grave," Frank told him the moment he arrived.

Seyi arched an eyebrow. "How possible is that? We've had two good days."

"Thanks to you!"

"We're moving to Oshogbo for the rest of the production," Asuka said. "Frank has guys checking out a suitable location."

Seyi gasped. "What about the interviews? And Oshogbo is not a part of Ijesaland, which is the focus of this episode."

"Well, this is no one's fault, Seyi." Frank scoffed. "Your king died." He clapped. "Let's get this shit rolling, guys! In the drawing room." He started walking away and yelled. "And Seyi, no babies to inspire you today, buddy. Get your inspiration somewhere."

Seyi rolled his eyes. "Talk to him, Asuka. It will be so unrealistic to go to the state capital when we are documenting these areas. The bulk of the gold we're talking about is around Ilesa. I only chose here because it's my home."

Asuka rubbed her arms. "Is Ilesa safe?"

"Their king is still alive."

Asuka chuckled. "Oh yes, of course."

The day was tough, but he forced his mind on it. After work, he stopped by Pade's office just for good measure. After their last meeting, he wasn't willing to speak about Nene or her work. But the only way he could know what was up was to go there. One of the young men who worked with Pade was closing from work. Seyi greeted but chose not to ask questions. Pade's car was outside, and a part of him hoped Nene was "cleaning" after work, as she said she did.

He went up a rickety staircase and knocked on a connecting door. He heard nothing and opened it anyway. He found Pade on the balcony, gazing into the dark night.

"I hear your father is going to be the next Olukoyi," Pade said. "Not only are you a rich boy, you'll be the prince."

Seyi snickered. "You may have your head chopped for saying that in public, Sly."

Pade arched an eyebrow. "By who? Ikoyi is a small town. With the way the Olori cried last night, the news was in the night market while Kabiyesi was still warm."

"The part of my father being king is–"

"Just another fact. He's next to the throne and we all know he was cheated last time." He moved toward the door leading inside his house. "She's not here, meanwhile."

Seyi frowned. "Your assumptions are ridiculous."

"You want her, don't you?" Pade came closer and thumbed his chest. "You are the biggest fool I have ever met, Iwaneye."

Seyi slapped his hand off. "Don't talk to me like that, Sly. Why did you employ her?"

"She's free. She needs to work, to look like a reputable member of society." Pade sniggered. "And her work is good. But it doesn't make her more acceptable. Exceptional with figures, and she keeps me so happy I don't miss Moni."

Seyi held back a punch. "I don't know why she agrees to such terms with you. She could go anywhere else."

"She can't. I don't believe she's a witch or anything. Just a girl with bad luck trailing her. Anything she touches destroys."

Seyi couldn't hold back the mean comment. "Like you?"

Pade shrugged. "That's why I keep her close. If she tries anything, I'll kill her."

Seyi breathed. "My mum believes she destroyed your marriage."

Pade frowned. "She asked my wife to leave me. What better way to destroy a person's home?"

Seyi shook his head. "For no reason? I don't believe that."

"Believe what you like." Pade went inside.

Seyi contemplated following him. Nene was not here, and he didn't want to hear more from Pade. The guy had so much bitterness in him, it weighed even on his walk. Seyi saw himself out, his head pounding. He drove back to the tree where he'd left Nene. The curfew would soon start, and he had to head back home. In a couple of days, the crew would move to the capital or Ilesa, if Asuka could convince Frank. There would not be time to make things right or see her again. If he left now, he would not want to come back...especially if his father became king. Those were not his goals, and he wasn't ready for small town fame.

He parked his truck in the same spot Nene showed him the day before, and walked the perimeter, hoping to find something. He felt rather than saw movement for a second and thought it could be a small bush animal. It was getting dark, but not dark enough to not see also a whiff of clothing. He followed the direction, and unknowing slid into a small pit.

"Ahhggg!" He grasped at the small plants within reach but they just came off in his hand.

Finally, his decline came to a stop. He rolled to his feet and found his Maxlite camping torch on his keychain. It wasn't so dark but this was a hole. Anything could be inside. He snapped on the torch and came face to face with Nene.

Seyi switched on a torch, jolting the darkness into illumine brightness. Her first instinct was to run further into the hole. She could hide, and he would never find her, but she stood stiffly, not even bothering to shield her face from his light. He stepped back for a second. She knew she should leave but couldn't. He'd try to follow and may get hurt. She was on her way to town before the curfew started to help with Mopelola's new baby, but now she couldn't. If she'd continued, he'd have spotted her on the road. Maybe she should have let him, and simply told him she had to go and help with the new mother.

He growled. "Are you not going to say anything?"

He slowly scanned the torch over her whole length. She was fully dressed in an old nightwear and her feet were covered neatly with an equally old wrapper. He took steps closer to her and touched her trim eyebrow. She didn't move, and he traced the paths on her smooth face. When he touched her soft lips, she flinched, and he snapped his hand back.

"What are you doing here?" He directed the torch to look around. "Inside a hole."

"You need to leave. Before the curfew starts."

"It's so dark here." He switched off his torch. "Why are you here?"

She could feel his breath on her face. Still, she refused to move. "Why? This is my hole. I live here."

"You live here," he mumbled. "You told me you live in Dada's compound."

"This is Dada's backyard," she said simply. "You need to leave. Vigilantes move around when the curfew starts."

He switched the torch back on. "What do you have here?" He pointed the light in different directions.

When on her own, she delighted in the fantasy of building a big house for herself and her children. Over the years, she had turned the gully behind Dada's house to her little mansion in the ground. To the outside world, it was a site destroyed by erosion and covered with bush, but once in the hole, it was her palace. Pieces of junk wood, leather, nails, and other leftover materials for caskets from the workshop found their way into her "house."

She was creative in her designs too. Seyi followed one of the narrow paths. The hole narrowed and caved in and she knew he could get hurt if he didn't bend as he proceeded. He was smarter than she thought and returned within a minute.

"I need some answers from you." He moaned. "First, do you just allow men to touch you as they wished?"

"I don't, what does that mean?"

"Because you stood still while I touched you just now. You enter this hole knowing I will follow you!" He breathed hard. "Where is this?"

"I wanted–" she moved a little more away from him. "What do you want?" She whispered.

"Answers." he snapped. "Why do you do it?"

She exclaimed. "Do what?"

"Strip men of their dignity. Tease them into submission. Spoil them with lust. Then you destroy their destiny."

"I don't know what you're talking about." Her voice cracked. She moved towards the small steps she'd carved to lead inside. "You need to leave now. They will see your truck and destroy it!"

He barked. "Adunola's husband!"

"Adunola's husband!"

Nene refused to answer any of his questions till he agreed to move the truck to a safe place since he wasn't leaving her. The implication of his decision stuck to his heart like a cancerous growth. His parents would be worried about his whereabouts. His mother would not bat an eye till he returned home. And for him, he'd be spending the night with a mysterious woman he admired and feared. Though he would never admit either even as he pondered on the truth.

"Get inside." He ordered after she pointed a big tree a few feet away where he could hide the truck from the main road. "I'm not going to risk you running into another hole when I can't follow you."

She didn't protest.

They came out of the truck and heard a man shout. "Who goes there?" The man came close holding a torch with bright lights.

Nene stiffened and grabbed his hand. She turned in the opposite direction a second before the vigilante saw them. If they'd gone the way they came, they'd bump into the watchman. Seyi had no idea where she was going but trusted her, and when she whispered, "Jump," while still holding his hand, he did.

They landed on the wooden ground with a loud thud, and she whispered, "Ssh." Another man joined the first and hushed voices made conversation as the men used what seemed like cutlasses to trash the bush. Then everywhere was silent.

"They've gone," Nene said. "Come this way."

She let go of his hand making him feel suddenly abandoned. Even in the dark, she knew her way through the gully, and shortly, they were back in the other hole. He switched on his torch.

"How many holes are here?"

"I don't know. They are not big."

"You should know. Why do you tell lies unprovoked?" He licked his lips. "I should have gone back before the curfew started." He didn't really mean that only wanted to see her reaction. She had none as he'd expected. and he pointed his light rudely on her face. "Where can I sit? I'm tired."

"Come." She turned to a really small looking hole and went on her knees. "Watch your head."

Chapter 14

T hey sat on two low stools in a small hole at the end of the narrow corridor they crawled through.

Seyi left his torch on and at first inspected the space, asking her several questions about where they were. She had discovered the space by accident, and seeing how hidden it was, made it her special space. The two sides of the "room" and the floor were padded with disjointed wood patterns, the work of someone skilled and creative, using bits of scrap hard, soft and plywood to make a design. What should have been a ceiling was a tent of tree branches with old clothes hanging on them. Besides the erosion, part of this gully had also been excavation sites of explorers looking for solid minerals.

A small shack was built with wood and raffia, and Seyi concluded she slept in there though a sleeping mat with strips of cloth trundled together to make a pillow lay rolled up against the shack. Clean, fresh, earthy smells permeated the air. Seyi imagined the trees provided shade and oxygen though he doubted they'd protect anyone from rain. He worried about insects but heard none buzz. He had so many questions to ask but the foremost on his lips wasn't even supposed to be his concern.

"Tell me about your relationship with Adunola's husband." Pade too, and Kunle, and any other men.

"He was actually a lusty man Adunola fell head over heels in love with." Nene avoided his gaze. "During their courtship years, he cheated on her on several occasions, arrogantly telling her off. But after an encounter that almost took his life, he humbly pleaded with Adunola to marry him and she gladly did." She took a deep breath. "They began to have problems with his commitment as he had begun to look out again. It was during that period he met me. Asked for my help."

"Why would he come to you?"

"I don't know. Adunola is my friend." She sighed. "I thought I could help him to overcome his lewdness and preached to him. Everyone started saying I was–"

He cut in. "What powers did you use on him to render him an invalid?"

"He has HIV. I didn't give it to him. But then, who would believe that?"

He snapped. "Not me either."

He wanted her so much and her aloofness drove him crazy. Maybe antagonizing her would help with his emotions.

"Adunola is my good friend now. When he started being sick, he confessed all to her and she came to apologise to me. And we are friends. He's really sick now."

"Mum said his condition worsens every day. Since Adunola confronted you."

"And she is right. But Adunola hasn't had the courage to tell anyone the cause of his illness. IT has nothing to do with me. I've told you before people see me as an easy excuse and I don't know why! Adunola herself–"

"Is positive?"

Nene nodded.

"There are drugs she could use if she checks in on time." Seyi looked away. "You should tell her."

"We will appreciate any help. She just got the courage to go to Ife for the test last week. She was perplexed," Nene said passionately.

The urgency in her voice drew Seyi's gaze back to her. "That doesn't mean you are no longer an ogbanje as you confessed," he said. "A witch that flies by the day."

She folded her arms and turned away. "You can believe whatever you want about me, I don't care."

He leaned forward and pulled her forcefully to face him and she snatched her arm from his grip. "You will look at me and care about my questions and inquiry," he said stiffly.

"Because I caused every evil in this town," she snapped. "Did Mum, tell you about all the other men I destroyed? Pade? And his father before him?"

"You tell me!"

"There's nothing to tell. People made their choices and they had nothing to do with me!" She stood, gathering her dress about her.

He stood too. "Then make me believe all are lies about you. That you do not destroy men in the invisible world before it translates to the physical."

She snickered. "And that I do not sleep with every one of them in their dreams before scattering their destinies. Or isn't that what everyone says? Isn't that what your mother has warned you against?"

"Isn't it true?"

She cried. "No, it is not."

"Then why have I been seeing you in my sleep. In my dreams, doing all the things you've been accused of and more!" he said softly.

She glared at him, her mouth dropped open. "I know it is not true," she whispered. "No man has ever confronted me with these accusations. It had always been their wives or mothers. Even Dada's wife accused me of spiritual incest."

He inhaled. "Incest?"

She breathed through her mouth. "I kiss you in your dream?"

"And more."

The air in the hole suddenly stilled. He reached out and pulled her into his arms, crushing her lips to his.

She pushed back and ran to the entrance of her shack. "I have never desired to do this. It is your imagination!"

"Why would I want to imagine that?" he picked the torch from the ground where he'd left it and directed it back on her face. "Look at you? You are nothing to be desired. A beautiful face and a body hidden by ugly clothing! Who knows what lay beneath, what you hide. Why would I imagine desiring you?"

"I can't imagine why," she said.

"You enjoy this, don't you?" he flipped the torch over her and returned it to her face. "You did it to my brother and he begged you several times to sleep with you in real life until your rejection drove him to suicide!" he barked. "You take delight in conquering young men."

"It's not true!" she screamed, her voice thick with emotion.

He watched her with mixed feelings. He could not afford to back down now. She was guilty. His mother had been right. She had powers and she had used them to manipulate as many men as she chose. Including him. He had to beat it. He had to win her.

"Explain this!" He threw the small scrapbook he had carried in his back pocket for days, at her, hitting her square on the face. The book fell to the ground and her gaze followed it. "Pick it up and explain it to me!"

She bent obediently and picked it, turning it in her hand. He had put her other picture in between, carrying it with him because he didn't want his mother to find it. Part of him knew she had seen it before and would want it. He meant to destroy it but couldn't. The words Kunle wrote in them had provided some reasons to why he took his life but had left the only suspect guiltless. Nothing in it indicted her. Anyone reading would say she was the only guiltless person in Kunle's life. He had desired her beyond reason; written genius poems in praise of her. He had lived for her! And it drove Seyi senseless.

Nene opened the folded scrapbook and the picture dropped out of it. She gasped, knowing the reason for Seyi's anger. It was the half nude picture of her! Half-nude not because she wore nothing but because of studio effects. Kunle had taken her to the photo studio of his friend's father in Ife to test some of the effects the studio could produce. One of it was to take the near-negatives of real people. The effect reduced the clothing to almost nothing. She had been shocked when she looked at the print and her breasts were almost as visible as there was no covering. She had pleaded with him to give her the 8x11 size picture printed with a grey scale effect which made it even more seductive. Nene herself had been told to throw her head back slightly, look as though she was sleepy, and asked to pout. The effect damaged the morals of any sane person seeing it. Her long natural hair had been scattered to create the desired blasting effect. She had pleaded with Kunle not to allow his friend to display it in their studio but had not had the courage to go back there to check. The only consolation was that part of her face had been hidden by shadows.

"Why did you allow him to take such a picture and refused to sleep with him?" Seyi yelled. "Why would you accept other men and not my brother?" He paced. "He loved you. He was crazy about you. He wrote poems about you. Talked about you in his private thoughts. Why would you not reciprocate?"

She breathed hard. "When I was eleven, a man came to our house with his mother. He was much older than me, of course. He was very big in my eyes. But ..." she looked at him and turned her back defiantly. "He was the most beautiful man I had ever seen in my life." Her voice trembled and caught in her throat, hoping to drive distraction far from him.

"They came to negotiate a casket. They didn't see me because I was working in the workshop."

She didn't know he had closed in on her until she felt his breath on her neck.

"You worked in the workshop? As what?"

"As a carpenter." She paused and swallowed to push away the bitterness she still felt when she thought or talked about her childhood.

Most of the injuries she had were now faint scars because of the beautiful quality of her skin. Some of them had been so ugly she'd thought they'd never fade.

"I couldn't stop looking at him that day. I had never felt like that about any man," she continued refusing to acknowledge his closeness in any way. "He didn't even see me. Besides, I was such a small child, thin and ugly, like everyone said. He couldn't have felt anything for me, anyway. But I never stopped loving him. Never could. I could never stop thinking about him.

She turned and fell into his arms. But he didn't touch her. In fact, he held the torch over his head so the light was on her face. She blinked. "He's the reason I couldn't love Kunle."

"Some stranger who didn't even know you! Please."

He stepped away from her as though she had an infectious disease and went back to take the low stool.

"Kunle's big brother." She sobbed. "He's Kunle's brother."

Chapter 15

S eyi's fingers remained braced, glued to the torch he held against her face.

He lowered the torch awkwardly. The confession knocked the breath out of him. Where had she gotten the courage from? But now he was the one feeling weak in his knees, unable to face her. He thought of what to do, give in, let her know how he felt? What feelings he fought day and night? He was an engaged man. If there was any time to stand for the woman he loved, it was now. But strength failed him.

She heaved a heavy sigh and looked down at her feet. "There, I have let it out. You can hate me like everyone else."

Her words jolted him out of his confused state. He raised the torch, and for a moment a blinding rage overwhelmed him. He couldn't control what his next action would be.

"How dare you?" He snarled. "Who are you to manipulate my brother and try to do the same to me."

He flung the torch at her, much the same way he threw the scrapbook at her. He knew it hit her though she didn't make a sound. The torch lay on the wooden floor facing him. She would see the anger and raw passion he couldn't seem to keep in check. Did she have a clue why he was so aggravated? The true reason?

"Answer me!"

"I did not manipulate–"

"Don't lie to me, damn you!" He leaped to his feet, shaking uncontrollably. "This is exactly what happened to Kunle. This is what my mother cried over, warned me about." He yelled. "You–"

"Your mother!" She shouted, cutting him off. "Your mother who nearly killed a pregnant woman out of jealousy. Your mother! Who cheated on your father out of revenge. Your mother–"

If she continued, he knew he would kill her. His feet did not listen to reason and his hands took matters on to themselves. He only found himself in front of her, his hands on her shoulders, shaking her slim body like that of a ragdoll.

"Shut up!" He screamed. "Don't say what you know nothing about."

He had to step away from her before he regretted his actions. She put up no defence of herself, but when she whimpered, "Kill me," he knew he had taken it too far.

He took a staggering step backward, letting go of her shoulders suddenly, and she slumped. Fear gripped his heart and he fell on his knees beside her.

"Nene! Nene!!" She didn't make a sound and he pulled her into a hug. Tears clogged his throat. "I'm sorry." He cupped her face and saw her eyes were open. "I don't know what's wrong with me."

"I'm sorry for shouting at you."

Seyi sat on the hard floor and cradled her.

Nene had often wondered why people reacted to her the same way, with extreme emotion. She tried to be less vocal over the years because it meant less pain. Still, there were times when she felt she didn't belong to the world and would rather be lost or disappear. It had never worked. She would leave. Go where the road led but someone would recognize her in the most unlikely place, and before she knew it, she'd be on her way back to Ikoyi. The farthest she ever got to was Akure a trip that took her a day and a night. She felt like leaving now.

She knew the day Seyi walked into town, she was on a countdown to trouble. What she least expected was the way his moods changed, and his anger terrified her. She wasn't even afraid so much of his fierceness, or the pain he had inflicted on her several times, hitting her, throwing things at her. Kissing her. Her greatest fear was the way she continued to want to be around him. Her hungry need to be accepted by him. She seemed alive only when he was with her, or around her, whether loving or hating her.

She needed to leave town for good.

For now though, she remained in his embrace, hating herself for wanting it. Anything to do with him would be met with stiff opposition by his family, and the entire community.

"What are you thinking?" he whispered.

"Nothing."

He moved her face closer. "Tell me."

"I don't belong here." She closed her eyes. "I want to die. Go to my mother."

He wiped sweat from her forehead. "Tell me about her."

She shook her head, unable to control the tears that slid down her cheek. "Hmm mmm."

Seyi's thumb caught one tear. He rubbed it around her cheek, massaging with a soothing round-and-round-the-circle.

"Where does she live?"

She shrugged. In truth, all she knew of her mother was the effigy she imagined spoke to her. Some of the time when she was so confused and frustrated, she talked to that beautiful woman she invented in her mind, and people called her a mad girl.

"Why don't you–"

"Because I don't know her."

He just never gave up. She detested the way he wanted to know everything about her. Everything. And she just would tell when he persisted. She sat up, and he didn't stop her. If she was going to talk about one of the deepest secrets of her life, then she wanted her own space, but she didn't stand. He was well within reach of hitting her or caressing her. His emotions swung like a hurricane, driving her to the edge of insanity, and extreme need. No one had ever made her feel this way, and she'd been to many edges and back.

"My mother died when I was a baby. My grandmother took care of me. She never talked about her daughter, and she shielded me from the mean things people said." She swallowed. To tell or not to tell. She decided to tell. "I was six when she died, and I was brought to live with my–"

Words never revealed. They thought she didn't know. But Ma'Nene told her before she died. Everything.

Seyi leaned forward. "Your?"

"Father. Idowu Dada." She got on her feet, a sudden fear of what he might do to her overwhelming her. "Of course, they didn't tell me. Made it look like a kind couple who wanted to help. But I knew." She heaved a heavy sigh. "He had an affair with my mother till his wife killed her."

The light from the torch seemed to have dimmed but she saw the look of disdain on his face.

"Small town secrets." He kissed his teeth. "I bet everyone knows."

Was this a good reaction or not? She didn't care, she continued. "You may be right. Mrs. Dada had not been able to conceive for her husband in ten years of marriage. People convinced her to accept me. A child brings a child, they said."

Seyi stood. She stepped away from him, busying herself by picking up the torch. "It's fading. We should turn it off to conserve it."

He took the torch from her and turned it off. "Mrs. Dada has six children," he said softly.

She scoffed. "They came like rabbits. At twelve I was babysitting six babies."

Chapter 16

"How old are you?"

"27."

Seyi whistled. "I would never have imagined. You look younger. Kunle would have been 28 now." The silence between them thickened. "Tell me about the last time you saw him."

Nene relished the darkness around her. How else could she recall? With Seyi so close, she felt her nerve end pulse. No one ever asked this question and though she had told it to her "mother" a million times, she was glad someone, Seyi especially, wanted the truth. Everyone had concluded Kunle killed himself for her just because he was at her place of work the same day. His mother too, along with Mrs. Dada had concocted their own tales.

"The vet clinic was new, and I had gotten a job there." She drew in her breath. "Every day was a task. The vet doctor was growing weary of all the tales about me." She moved away from him. "I'm sorry, I'm not making any sense. Anyway, on that day, Kunle came in. Said your mum needed rat poison and didn't want to come in herself."

"Did he say why?"

She noticed he had moved away too. His voice seemed as though coming from the other side of the gully.

"No. And I didn't ask."

"Go on."

"We didn't sell rat poison. At first, I asked him to go to the chemist. Then the vet doctor came in and told me we had a stock he wanted to test and see if it was good. They are like pellets, and smell like chocolate."

Seyi snapped. "That would have made it easy for Kunle to swallow."

Nene leaned against the entrance of her shack. If he moved any closer with that edge she recognized in his voice, she was going to enter her shack and disappear through a hole she had in there. He would never find her. No one would. It was a final decision. If she left, she'd made sure they never saw her again. All the things she feared no longer existed; being alone, earning a living, surviving...she was no longer a child, and Nigeria was big enough.

"The vet doctor was willing to give him for free. He was the first to get it." Nene licked her lips. "Kunle stared at him. There was something."

"Did he say anything after the vet gave him, any hint he wanted it for himself?" Seyi sounded closer to her and she shuddered. He didn't touch her though.

"The vet gave it to me and told me to make sure I follow up. He was new in town, didn't really know many people." She sighed. "I gave Kunle. And he didn't hint anything. Thanked me."

"And left? What was his mood like? You said there was something with the way Kunle stared?"

"I couldn't place it but something was not right. The vet doctor only came into the front office briefly, and there was an exchange between him and Kunle." She sighed. "Kunle wanted to sleep with me. That was what he said...the last thing he said to me was silly. Made no meaning till later."

"What was the last thing he said to you?"

"So you mean I'll die without kissing you." Nene closed her eyes, remembering the following morning when Mrs. Dada came into the vet to accuse her. She needed some answers as well. "Did he leave a suicide note, do you know?"

"A suicide note?" He switched on the torch but pointed it to the floor. "Why do you ask?"

He was a few feet away, directly in front of her. Too close for her comfort. "Mrs. Dada came into the vet the following morning, weeping. She was just from your house. The whole of Ikoyi got the news in the morning. And she came to accuse me. I lost my job. By evening, I was run out of town." She scoffed. "Much the same way they beat a witch out of the village in those days. With sticks and stones."

"Come here." Seyi reached out and pulled her into his arms.

She let him, fighting tears. "The vet also left, I heard when I came back."

Seyi massaged the tense muscles of the back of her neck. "Kunle didn't leave a note. But I suspect my mother found some poems he wrote for you and drew her conclusions."

"He sometimes said some words to me." She raised her head to look up at him. "I swear, I never encouraged him to have feelings for me."

"Growing up, Kunle was Mum's favourite. I was Dad's." Seyi held her gaze. "We were never close as brothers should be. And when he died, I blamed myself. I was glad I wasn't home. I didn't want to know anything about it, and that guilt ate at me all these years."

It made no sense she wanted to let out everything to him, but she couldn't beat the feeling out of her system.

"I feel cheated." She moved out of his embrace again. And he let her. "I want to fight back. Why would I be blamed for everything? My life was hard enough."

"They say success is the best form of revenge. Succeed. And you have your revenge."

"I can also run like I always do. No one will ever find me."

"When did you come back to Ikoyi? And why?"

"I was 17." She couldn't stop her tears anymore and they trickled down her face. "I walked to the nearest village and slept by the road. I don't know how I survived. But I had nothing. After a week, I found my way back, and hid in the bushes during the day."

"You did not deserve to be treated that way." He moved closer. "I guess I can't imagine what life has dealt you, but you can move on with your life. Do other things."

She snickered. "That's what I decided. Just like my grandmother did before she died. Spill the beans. No use taking secrets to the grave."

He pulled her back into his arms. "Don't talk about dying. You have a lot to live for."

"I do?" Her head felt light. "What do you mean by a lot? I live here in a hole like a rat." Hysteria threatened to take over. "I don't earn money. I live on charity."

"Then why do you stay here? You are no longer 17. You can go anywhere else. You speak well, at least you got a job with Pade." He cupped her face. "What are you not telling me?"

"Everything."

"Then tell me everything, Nene. We have all night," he whispered against her ear.

What did she have to lose?

His head warned he played with fire, but his heart would not let him leave her. He had never felt so drawn to anyone, not even Jenrola. Nene was a mystery to him, he couldn't let go until he unraveled her. There was no point in doing anything else. He was stuck here in this hole with her. The cool breeze outside blew the branches of the trees which made up of their roofing, releasing small wisps of fresh air. He could cuddle for a long sleep, but her words entranced him. Common sense told him he wasn't ready to hear "everything." But his human nature walked her to the sleeping mat where his body spooned hers.

At this point, he felt more romantic than was good for both of them, but he would never force her to do anything. Her morals proved to be higher than anyone had given her credit for and if indeed she was the seductress they made her out to be, then it was too late for him to escape her trap. He waited for her to unleash. In the meanwhile, he wanted her to trust him. Her braced profile provided a thick wall she put up between them. Though he continually drew her back to him, he could feel the way her heart thudded, and her arms and shoulders stiffened at his every touch. If she hadn't confessed her infatuation, he would continue to believe she didn't want him. Again, it was so long ago. She didn't mention she was still captivated.

"Tell me, Nene. Please." He wound his arms around her waist and rested his chin on her temple. "You know I am involved now."

Her voice was low. "From the beginning?"

"Everything."

"There are a lot of secrets." She turned slightly. "You will hate me...about the people you love?"

He sensed her hesitation, could understand how she must feel. "Then it will remain between us." Binding, he thought.

"I know my story and I think many people do too. I am the Cinderella, living with a helpless father and a wicked stepmother. The only difference is that I am not a daughter in the house, but a liability. A bastard child. A charity case who happens to know too much."

Chapter 17

"Nene!"

"Nene!"

The voice came from somewhere far and she groaned. Seyi stirred and lifted his head. He checked his watch, careful not to disturb Nene whose head lay on his chest. It was too early to wake after such a long night, though now getting too late to start the day. He hadn't checked the time when she finally stopped talking, but it couldn't have been more than an hour ago.

Nene opened her eyes. "Mrs. Dada is calling me."

"She is there." Mrs. Dada seemed so close now. "If she's not in this one, she'll be in the next one."

"Ah, Mrs. Dada! Help me. My son did not sleep in his bed last night." A woman screeched. "I'm done. My own is finished. Mrs. Dada don't stand and stare at me like this."

"Ssh." Seyi put a finger to Nene's lips. "My mum is with her." He sat up and drew Nene with him.

"Carol, calm down. We are not even sure he is here."

"Where will he be? Ehn? Everybody has been seeing them together. They were on his set together, and they were at Mrs. Bello's." Carol seemed to stomp her feet, or maybe she slumped on to the hard ground. Seyi had no way of knowing, but the ground vibrated.

"Making a scene in my backyard is not going to change anything if he's with her, Carol. I will leave you here o! Let me call her out." Mrs. Dada raised her voice. "Nene! I know you're there. Come out."

Seyi shook his head, and mouthed, "No."

"Let me go, Seyi. You need to leave too." Nene heaved. "After all you know now, you should go back to Lagos, and marry your girlfriend. You have no business here."

"Lower your voice," Seyi said softly. "We'll leave together. I just need to get home and clean up. You too. Then we can go to the set and plan everything else."

"They are talking!" Mrs. Dada shouted. "Nene! Nene! Nene! How many times did I call you?" A string of invocations followed on a background of Carol's sobbing.

Seyi flew to his feet. "Is she making incantations? Casting a spell on us?"

"They can't touch you. It's me she wants."

He grabbed her hand. "Let's get out of here."

She didn't protest as they half-ran to the truck and got in. He knew she would not utter a contrary word even if she disagreed. The drive to his home took a little longer because of the back road that led to Nene's holes. At his home, he parked his truck by the gate, which made them walk right through the front part of the sitting room to get to the back door. It would be locked but he had a spare key.

They made it into his room without any event.

"The bathroom is over there." He pointed. "Take a bath."

He opened his unpacked suitcase and brought out a pair of jeans and tees. It would be too big for her, but that would be taken care of. The costumes woman on his set would get her size and do some shopping.

"Thank you." She collected the clothing and entered the bathroom.

Seyi stared after her, his heart beating hard against his chest. He hadn't told her yet, but he'd decided she was going with him to Lagos. He would not be able to live without her. Though they met barely a week ago, now his life was in her hand. Literally. He picked out something to wear as well, then went in search of his father. As of the moment, he had nothing to say to his mother. Nene had told him a lot about his parents' "sick" marriage that made more sense than he cared to think about. He wasn't going to process anything here or he'd be doing something worse than Kunle did.

Chief Iwaneye sat on the edge of his bed when Seyi knocked and entered. He prostrated in the traditional manner of greeting and sat beside him.

"I was coming to your room to talk to you." Chief smiled. "How was your night?"

Needless to say he didn't sleep much, or that he wasn't in his bed over the night, Seyi smiled back. "It was good, sir." Obvious his father didn't know he wasn't home over the night. Probably didn't care too.

"The family decided I will be the next king. The other ruling house will present their candidate of course, but you know how it is done." The old man raised two thick fingers. "Two-two."

"I know, Daddy." Seyi sighed. "What do you think about that?"

"I want it." Chief shrugged. "It's the only reason I stayed back here and not pursue a better career in Lagos or Ibadan. Your great-great-grandfather was Olukoyi, and since then, our family has been bequeathed the throne. But the family grew large and brothers fought themselves. I'm glad I am the preferred candidate now."

Seyi gasped. He never knew this. "I–I'm happy the opportunity finally is here."

"Yes, Seyi," Chief grunted. "So, how's your production going?"

"My director is moving it to Osogbo. With the curfew and all, he wants to be able to work late."

"Sorry to hear that. It was good to have you back home."

"I wanted to let you know I won't come back here after work today. We'll just go to Osogbo after closing the site." Seyi itched to say more. But wasn't sure his mother would not come home before he left.

"Huh, well, that's okay. I hope you'll come for the coronation. If I am crowned."

"Definitely Daddy. Wherever I am in the world, I will bring myself here." He stood. "I have to run now."

Chief stood too. "Thank you. If you know how to pray, please do. It will be a long battle because the other family wants it badly too."

"It's usually like that." Seyi hugged his old man. "I'll call later in the evening."

"Have you told your mother? I don't know if she's awake yet."

"Help me tell her." Seyi hurried out. If Chief didn't know his wife was not home, then he wasn't going to be the talebearer.

What Nene told him about his parents shook him to the roots, but those were details he may never act on. Of what use would it be? Secrets forever buried hurt no one.

Nene opted to use the bucket and bowl rather than the shower. That way, she conserved water, a force of habit. The water was cold against her skin and refreshing, but she didn't want to indulge. Seyi didn't tell her his plans and she didn't want to be the cause for delay. She should ask, but she'd learned a long time ago never to ask questions.

As she soaped with his body wash, her mind roamed to the night before. Seyi had been a gentleman. She knew how much he fought his desires, several times especially the hour they were both supposed to be asleep, he touched her inappropriately. She liked it too. Too much. Something changed in their relationship, but she didn't want to put her mind to it. Everything she told him during the night was true. Did he believe her? He made no indication. At least he seemed to still want her around. And because bringing her into his house was not a good idea, she planned to be discreet. Panicked, she would not let it show. If she could just get by this day, she would be fine.

Once upon a time, she would die to have Seyi Iwaneye smile at her, touch her. Now, she just wanted to live a peaceful life. She had finally conceded defeat to the forces of Ikoyi, and especially Mrs. Dada, the town witch. Though Mrs. Dada made it clear Nene was the evil one. They did not succeed in killing her, which she doubted was part of the plan. Drive her crazy, maybe. Like Atarodo, a once famous madwoman who lived in a small abandoned shed for decades, they wanted her to be the shame of the town, the laughing stock.

No one thought she was normal. No one associated with her in daylight. Their extra chores she could do when no one saw her with them, and they knew to call on her in their emergencies. They only used her, and the more she was forced to see herself as she was, and as they treated her, the more she despised her existence. People didn't think she had human feelings, well how could they. How could anyone go through what she'd been and be sane?

She heard a door open and froze. He was back. Probably needed to use the bathroom. She threw the last two bowls of water over her back and dried off quickly. Within a minute, she had on his shirt and jeans. The smell of him overwhelmed her and she dragged in a deep breath. A temptation she dared not fall into. It would be the most devastating experience of her life if she fell for him, and he ditched her, or worse, didn't give her a try! Even worse, wanted her only for his physical satisfaction. She didn't trust the system, she trusted no one with her heart. They had broken it so many times some assumed she didn't have one. Despite Seyi's kindness all through the night, she feared he only wanted to unravel her, and then join the forces to destroy her. In the past, she withstood anyone and anything they did to her because she didn't care.

Seyi was different. She cared.

Nene opened the bathroom door, clutching her old clothes. She wanted to apologize for taking so much time, but words failed her. Carol Iwaneye stood in the middle of the room her eyes wild with mischief and fury, and emotions Nene lacked words to describe.

"What are you doing here?" She screamed. "Yee! Someone help me!" She clasped her hand over her head and wailed.

Nene didn't know her way around, but she could find out. She rushed to the door, but Carol followed and dragged her back with such force, she fell on her butt.

Carol wailed, stomping her feet. "Daddy! Daddy! The witch is here. Somebody help us ooo!"

Nene swallowed. If Seyi didn't come to her rescue, they may beat her to death here. After last night and the way he touched, and cuddled her, had he lured her here to avenge his brother? She had to find a way out. She couldn't trust anyone. She stood in one swift movement. There were only two doors – the exit and the bathroom. Carol blocked the exit and was now armed with a foot of Seyi's big boots. Though the older woman was slight, Nene wasn't willing to tackle her. She went for the bathroom instead and locked herself in.

Carol banged on the door while Nene assessed the window. She went to the only small window available. It wasn't only too small, she couldn't open it. She felt trapped.

A small noise distracted her, and she returned to the door and pressed her face to the keyhole. Seyi was back, pushing his mother out of the room. The two spoke rapidly, harsh words repeated with knowing undertones.

"Get out of my room, Mama Kunle!"

"Oh, because I'm trying to save you from a witch I am now Mama Kunle?" Carol shouted. "Are you so bent on being destroyed?"

"You think I don't know you, Mrs. Iwaneye? That Kunle is not your husband's son? That you cheated on him." Seyi yelled. "Who are you to judge anyone?"

Nene closed her eyes. Not here, not now, Seyi!!!

Carol whimpered. "Seyi? Who fed you with such lies?"

"Get out of my room and keep your face out of my business!"

Nene heard the door slam and slumped against the door.

Seyi knocked on the bathroom door. "Nene. Open up. Let's go."

She unlocked the door and fell into his arms, sobbing. "I'm sorry. I didn't mean–"

"It's okay. I shouldn't have brought you here." He patted her back. "I'll just grab my stuff. I can clean up on set."

Chapter 18

Nene climbed up the hole and pushed branches back to break into the backyard of Idowu Dada's compound.

"Let her son go. The woman has suffered enough." Mrs. Dada spat. "Showing yourself to me doesn't stop my charms from working."

Nene stepped forward, careful not to tread on poison she perceived would be on the ground. She had to remove her hand chisel from the carpentry workshop. Otherwise, nothing would have brought her back here. It was a special one, a gift from an old man who Dada later made his coffin, and she knew she'd need it sometime soon. Even if she didn't, it was special to her. The only thing anyone ever gave her in her adult life. A reminder of her life's journey.

"I am talking to you!"

"Mrs. Dada, I have heard you." She disappeared into the workshop and found the tool.

"This is the last time you'll eat a man like that. Temitope's blood cries against you!" Mrs. Dada followed her. "Where is Carol's son, witch? A-je! Bring out the woman's son now before I scream this town on your head!"

Nene walked out. "It's what you do best."

Regardless of Seyi's plans, she was done here. One more shot, and if things didn't work out, she'd do the last thing on her mind. No one knew this, but she carried a sachet of the rat poison that killed Kunle Iwaneye in her shack. It was the only thing she took with her from the vet. With ten years on its potency, an expired rat poison would definitely do a better job than a good one.

Nene jumped rather than climb down and stood in the hole gathering her emotions. It was over she kept telling herself. She walked out the other side where Seyi waited in his vehicle.

He caressed her cheek. "Did you get what you wanted?"

"Yes, thank you," she murmured.

"Everything will be okay, I promise you." He put the truck in gear. "Frank called already. I'm late."

She averted her gaze, so he won't see her tears. "Thanks for coming over."

What difference did it make? She was just as scared as the first day Mrs. Dada raised a spatula on her, weeks into her first pregnancy. Nothing much had changed in her story. It was still the merry-go-round of a rejected motherless baby.

Seyi was quiet through the short drive, which she was grateful for. In her mind, she believed she had said all there was to say. Right now, she only waited for nothing. A hopeless person seemed better off than her.

The production set was busy when they arrived. Seyi parked beside his cabin just like the last time and hurried out of the truck.

"I just need you to stay here, or you can come and watch production." He preceded her into the cabin. "I'll have Asuka send the costume lady over."

She looked around the neatly furnished cabin. She never imagined it looked so nice inside. "Costume?"

"Yes. You need clothes." He arched an eyebrow. "Remember?"

A soft knock and a voice came through. "May I come in?"

"Yes. That's Iyabo, my set assistant."

Iyabo opened the door. "Good morning." She only spared Nene a quick glance but she felt the lady's eyes ate her up.

I shouldn't be on edge like this. The worst is over.

Seyi pulled out clothes from a small wardrobe and checked through sheets of paper, moving around the small cabin. "I'll be ready in ten minutes. Find Asuka to find the costumier. I need some clothes for Nene."

Iyabo looked at her again. "Okay. The morning meeting was just about to finish. I saw your truck come in."

Seyi swirled past and entered what Nene assumed was the bathroom. She sat on a chair, suddenly feeling a heavy burden on her heart.

Iyabo folded her arms across her chest. "You were here two days ago with the school."

It was a question though. Nene shrugged. She didn't answer assumptions. Iyabo had been harmless then but didn't seem so this time.

"Well, let me tell Asuka about you." Iyabo left.

Nene wanted to know who Asuka was but it could wait. She was on a default mode, awaiting judgement. Till she was told the whole plan, she just wanted to have no thoughts.

Seyi walked out of the bathroom in a deep blue bathrobe, dripping water. He looked so adorable and smelt fresh. She didn't want to notice him, but he walked over and pulled her into his arms.

"I'll take care of you. Okay?"

She nodded, overwhelmed. Still afraid, and unsure.

"It's going to be quite busy today. Don't be shy. If you need me, come over to me. Okay?" She nodded. He cupped her cheeks. "If you need anything, ask Iyabo or Asuka. Anyone. Even Frank. Hmm?"

"Yes, thank you."

He gazed at her mouth for lasting several seconds then tilted her head and took possession of her mouth in a heated kiss. A soft knock, much like the earlier one tore them apart.

He called. "I'll be out in a minute."

"Asuka said we'll go shopping once recording starts," Iyabo said.

He raised his voice. "Good. I'll be done in a minute." Seyi pressed a kiss on Nene's lips. "You'll be in good hands, okay?" He murmured and pressed another kiss to her mouth. And another. Then laughed. "I can continue all day."

Nene drew in a shuddering breath as he stepped away and got dressed. He wasn't modest, and she had to turn away to avoid being caught staring.

When he was ready, he walked over to her again and kissed her. His lips caught hers in a gasp of delight. She moaned softly and opened her mouth to his invitation. He devoured her. She clutched his jeans, which she wore, with both hands in order to steady herself from the onslaught. He gripped the back of her head with one hand while the other dropped from her waist to cup her hip. They were both lost in their passion for several minutes, gasping for air and taking more of each other, but then he disengaged and rested his forehead on hers and she soon realized why.

His phone rang a unique tone. He pushed away slowly and removed it from the pouch in his front pocket.

"Yeah, hello. Jenny?" he walked towards the bathroom door, avoiding her dazed look.

He must have put it on speaker because she heard the conversation clearly. His girlfriend, Jenny. Did he do this on purpose? She turned her back to give him privacy and gather her thoughts.

"Honey, I am so sorry for earlier on," Jenny said rather breathlessly. "I just left a meeting now, can you believe that?"

"It's alright. I just wanted to say hello."

"Are you okay, darling. You sound...breathless," she said.

"Yeah. I'm alright." He took a deep breath. "So, what was the meeting about?"

"If hell was not going to be let loose. We had a robbery in the bank...No one was hurt but the men were armed." She sighed. "God, it's been a hell of a day."

"You don't mean that!" He exclaimed. "Are you sure you're alright?"

Nene clenched her teeth. She didn't want to hear his conversation with his lover.

"Yes. Five of them walked in dressed like women. They were armed to the teeth."

He gasped. "What happened to the metal detectors in the doors?"

"Hell, if I know. The doors were bad. The security men held the doors open for customers. I'm sure they had to do with it. One of them just announced that a robbery was about to take place. They brought out very sophisticated handguns. Shot twice into the roof, it caved in. Everyone cooperated after that." She sighed again.

"I'm so sorry. Are you sure you're alright?"

"Yes darling, thank God no one was hurt. Carted away about three million only, thank God. They came in after that call of yours while I was trying to investigate a transfer one of my staff made without due approval."

"What a day for you. So early too. You should go home."

"No. We closed to customers though. The police are here."

"You need to go home and rest–"

"I will. I'll call you when I get home."

"Okay then. Be safe, darling."

"You too. I love you," she said. He hung up without reiterating.

He walked to her and brought her to face him with both hands. "Sorry, that was–my fiancée."

She continued to stare blankly at him.

"I mean my girlfr–"

"I know what a fiancée means. I am not a prostitute."

"Of course not." He traced her lower lip with his thumb.

She jerked out of his reach. "Don't touch me. I mean nothing to you. I am just a wayside, village girl. But I will not be treated like a prostitute because I am not one."

"I won't treat you like a prostitute. I never have and never will."

"You think," she breathed hard. "I don't know what you think? You touch me anyway you like, and I allow you, then you keep your fine lady and treat her with respect."

He exclaimed. "I treat you with respect! What's this, Nene? What's this drama for?"

"If what you do to me is respect, then I wonder what you do when you disrespect someone." She picked the nylon bag with her dirty dress and stepped around him, her movement jerky.

"What was I supposed to do when she called? Was I supposed to–? What do you think you're doing?" He turned to look at her.

She yelled. "I'm going back to my shack!" She grabbed the door handle.

"You'll stay here." He pulled her back toward the fancy couch. She staggered but he paid no attention. "We'll talk about this later." He snatched a file off a side table. "I'll send Asuka." He slammed the door behind him.

Chapter 19

Nene lowered herself to the couch, holding her middle.

This was the exact reason she kept to herself. She was like fodder for the wicked mind. Why was she such as easy prey? How would she ever survive in this world? Maybe she should make a dramatic exit since Seyi seemed to need some drama. She opened the nylon bag and took out the sachet of rat poison. If she swallowed all and locked herself in his bathroom, they'd be too late to pump her by the time she was found. She blinked several times. This was it. Time to take a bow and leave peace in the world. No one would miss her...well, admit to missing her. They'd be glad she was finally gone, the voice of their consciences. But in their hearts, they'd know the truth, and that was good enough.

The door opened, and she froze the sachet in her clutch.

A petite Asian woman walked in. She fixed her eyes on Nene, and Nene jumped to her feet, the nylon and sachet still in her grip.

The woman smiled. "Relax. I'm Asuka. You're–"

"My name is Nene."

"Seyi's princess." She laughed. "Forget I said that. We're leaving for the market once the make-ups are done and the costumier can get away." She moved closer to Nene. "Seyi has reported himself. Men are so naughty."

Nene swallowed. What did she mean by "reported himself?" Did he kiss and tell? Her stomach turned. One new hater born. What would the woman think of her? Another thing bothered her. The market. She couldn't go to the market. She never did, especially in broad daylight.

"Come on, sit down, relax." She patted the space beside her on the couch. "The twins are make-up artist and costumier. I can't tell them apart, so I just call them Ejire."

Nene arched an eyebrow. Asuka was sure something. To know to call the twins Ejire was interesting. If she wasn't so racially Asian, one would not know by her name or accent. She spoke like a Nigerian through and through. Nene liked her at once, her bane.

She took the seat Asuka offered.

"They're very good too. Seyi wants them to give you a makeover." Asuka used her hand to brush Nene's hair back. "You are so pretty."

The very thought scared the daylight out of her. "I don't want a makeover."

"Looks like you don't have a choice now. The guy is gung-ho." She giggled. "The last time I saw a man stupefied like this over a woman was when my husband met me." She winked. "Aren't I just funny."

Nene twisted her fingers. Nothing was funny if Seyi already gave off this kind of impression. There were locals on the set. They would go back home and paint the picture they wanted. The story would be she had eaten Mrs. Iwaneye's second son too.

"He is engaged," she muttered.

"And I reminded him too." Asuka clapped. "Any-who! Let's talk about your style. I hope you like colour. Feminine. Something beautiful like you."

Like an iron rod poked her from behind, Nene leaped to her feet. "They don't sell those things in Ikoyi."

"I was told there's a lot of lovely fabric here. We can buy what we need and when we get to Osogbo, get them sewn." Asuka rose slowly. "Just till we return to Lagos."

"I'm not going to Lagos." Nene stepped away. "I don't need new clothes."

Asuka gave her a thorough physical appraisal and she could imagine what went on in her mind. "You remind me of myself. So afraid to trust anyone. I understand you perfectly."

The door opened and Seyi walked in his face all powdered up. Nene's heart skipped several beats. He kept his gaze on her though he spoke to Asuka. She couldn't read his expression. Was he still angry?

"The driver is ready. I thought I'd come and tell you myself."

Asuka sighed. "Aren't you doing any recording today?"

"Just one scene then we pack up. We should all be out of here before four." He looked at the nylon and sachet she still gripped. "You may have to buy two or three dresses only. Just to get by the next few days."

She wanted to tell him she didn't want any clothes, or to go to the market or to have a makeover. Or go to Lagos. She said nothing.

"Are the twins ready now, any of them?"

"Frank thinks you all can't leave. I'd rather have you go with her, Asuka," Seyi said.

Asuka rolled her eyes. "Huh, how sweet."

Seyi took the sachet and nylon from her hand and stared at them for a moment. "You won't need these."

Her mouth dropped open. "I want my tool."

"Tool? Seyi didn't tell me you work with tools." Asuka elbowed him with a smile. "And I think you told me every-thing."

Nene clenched her teeth to keep from talking. She really wanted to run out the door. "I'm a carpenter. Maybe he was ashamed to say that. But I like the job." She breathed in. She had said too much already. "It makes me creative." She licked her lips. "My tool, please?"

He looked in the bag and gave her. "You two have fun." He stomped out.

"Nerves. Calm them all down." Asuka took her hand. "See chemistry, though."

The atmosphere was tense on the set as well. The men worked with precision. Frank gave short sharp commands and spared no mistakes. Seyi couldn't stop thinking about Nene and couldn't bring himself to concentrate, but he was a professional. He could speak and think. One of the leading soft-sell magazines had compared him to a smooth operator. Never ruffled by anything. Till now, though. Nene was driving him nuts. He couldn't remember any time he had been this horny in his life or needing someone so badly. He shouldn't have picked up that call from Jenny but it had come at a time he needed to step away. He'd used Jenny when he didn't think he had any control left.

He felt like a real jerk.

"Alright, we're done here!" Frank yelled. He started clapping and grinned. "Good job, guys!" He hit Seyi on a shoulder. "You come through. Great job!"

Seyi smirked. "Thanks, bud."

"Let's pack up, now! Time to go."

Seyi looked around and muttered to no one in particular. "These women should be back."

Nene continued to hold back but he couldn't wait to win her, have her love him, lose control in his arms. She had started kissing him back when Jenny's call came through. He dragged in a wisp of air through his mouth. He strode towards his cabin. He needed to busy himself with packing up. He had a life to live. Frank had laid out an agenda. They would conclude the recording in a few days and return to normalcy in Lagos. His life was just as busy when he was recording as when he wasn't. There were shows, presentations, and he just auditioned to present for a continental game show. A lot was up, and he wanted to focus. Nene was coming with him to Lagos, then he'd sort her out.

As for Jenny, there was nothing there for him. She was a great girl, career-driven, fun and passionate about him but he wasn't feeling it anymore, and this made him question if ever there was anything to feel in the first place. Nene filled his view again, and his heart thudded. Until he explored what was there, he would not know. And now he wanted to settle down, have a woman in his bed every night, make babies...with Nene.

Iyabo knocked softly and entered without invitation. "Your mum is here."

Seyi rolled his eyes and continued taking his personal items off the room and into his open suitcase. There were not many things to pack but he sorted through sheets of paper and little items like extra clothing.

"Do you want to see her here or in the drawing room?" Iyabo put an empty disposable plate in the dustbin. "I can finish clearing up here."

"I'll see her in the drawing room, thanks."

Iyabo nodded and left. He took in several deep breaths and went followed.

Several people worked feverishly to tidy up. The truck with their equipment was almost all loaded. Frank stood by his cabin, staring into space like he did when he tried to internalize situations. Something must be up. Seyi wondered why Asuka and Nene were not yet back. It had been four hours at least since they went to the market.

"Mum, hello."

Carol turned. She had stood in the empty room, her back to the door, staring at nothing but steel walls.

"Seyi dear. I came to apologize." She clasped her hands. "I was just so shocked you could bring that–person into our house. I–"

He clenched his teeth. Did his mum just pretend as if she didn't know Nene's name? "It's okay, Mum. If that is all, I'll like to return to work."

"You don't seem to understand who this person is. She–"

"Her name is Chinenye. Call her Nene if you like."

"You–" Carol swallowed. "She told you her full name? You've been spending time with her?"

Seyi growled. "I know who you have been spending time with. Mrs. Dada. Who chants incantations every turn she gets but leads Sunday School every week."

"You have no idea what Mrs. Dada has been through with that girl. And how supportive she has been of our family."

"She has been supporting you, Mum. I know that much." Seyi paced. He knew it was time to stop but he couldn't. "When you are with Kunle's father, she covered up for you!"

"That is not true. Your father is Kunle's father." Carol screamed. "That girl has been feeding you with lies. She-"

"You don't even know how to lie. The genotype. Mine, yours, Daddy's, Kunle's."

"Seyi, please stop this. Your father cheated on me from day one. Did that little witch tell you about-"

"Mopelola, my sister. You almost killed her. When her mother was pregnant for her. That's why she was born crippled."

Carol glared at him and he glared right back. "Well, it is obvious you have been in bad company, and I cannot blame you. This is what I warned you about." She drew in a shuddering breath. "Please come back home. I am sorry about what happened this morning."

"We're moving production to Osogbo. I'll go to Lagos from there."

"Please Seyi. What happened, long ago. With Kunle and the family. I am sorry."

"It's okay, Mum." He sighed. "I just want to move on with my life."

"Stay away from her. She spews poison-"

"I need to get back to my cabin. We are packing and will need to leave before the curfew starts."

"Will you come for the coronation, your father's—"

"Did Kunle know his father?"

Carol pressed her lips together. She opened her mouth twice and closed them right back. "He—I didn't—"

Iyabo barged into the drawing room sweating and shaking. "Asuka came back. Please come."

Seyi ran out and found Asuka hurrying towards him. "I don't know where she is. We looked everywhere. She ran. She ran so fast."

Seyi gripped her shoulders. "Calm down, Asuka. What happened?"

Tears streamed from Asuka's eyes. "We got to the market. She wanted to stay in the car, but I encouraged her to come with me. It's a small market." She breathed. "Someone called her name very loud. And that's how it started. They stepped out from their shops. Screaming. I didn't know what to do, what was happening."

"Then she started running?"

"Yes. She turned and started running away. She didn't go back to the car. I called and followed her. And people followed her. They were throwing stones and sand at her." Asuka sobbed. "I was so confused."

Seyi rushed towards his cabin. He knew where she'd go. Asuka hurried after him. He found his keys and sunglasses.

"I'll find her." He brushed past her and bumped into his mother. "Excuse me."

"You're not going after her, Seyi, please."

"Excuse me, Mum." Seyi glared down at Carol. "I don't want to have to push you."

"Let her be, please." Carol cried. "How can a whole town detest someone, and you want to go after her. Is it normal?"

She turned to Asuka. "Please stop him. That girl eats people's destinies. See what she is doing to him now."

"Excuse me." Seyi shoved Carol and stomped out of the cabin.

Chapter 20

S eyi knew where to check first.

He parked under the hidden tree. It was still a couple hours before the curfew. He planned to convince her to come with him. He would drive directly to Osogbo. Iyabo could handle moving his stuff. He had the address of the hotel the crew would use, and he would find his way there. First was to find Nene. He took out the torch and extra batteries. He always had them with him. Living in Lagos called for many emergency measures.

Inside, he switched on the torch and found Nene crouched in a corner. She didn't even go deeper into the hole where her shack was. She had changed into one of her long dreary dresses. Her face was awash with tears. He lowered the torch and dropped to his knees in front of her.

"I'm sorry." He reached out to touch her, but she recoiled. "You have every right to be upset. I wasn't thinking." She sniffed, and he took out his handkerchief. "Here. Take." She didn't respond.

Water pooled in her eyes and Seyi wanted to lick them. He moved closer. "Nene let's go. I won't stop anywhere. We'll drive straight to Osogbo. To the hotel, we're lodging at. If you don't want to see anybody I'll make sure–"

She went on all fours and crawled into the hole.

Seyi sighed. "Nene." He sat back on his heels and pondered. "Nene come out." She was quiet. "Are you going to be running every time?" No response. "Do you want me to come and drag you out of there?"

He crawled through the small passage. When he was in the other hole, he turned on the torch.

"Nene?"

It was empty. He should have known to follow her immediately. Would he continue to make silly mistakes! The hole space was just a standard room size, with the tent-sized shack against the back wall. Seyi flipped the torch all over but she wasn't there. He walked to the shack and opened its wooden door.

"Nene?"

He moved the torch over the space inside, his heart beating so fast. He never imagined there would be anything inside except for a mat, and probably her clothes. What he saw got him gasping. And Nene was nowhere in sight. There were two passages that led away from inside though, and he followed them one at a time, calling her name. The two led nowhere, and he returned to the shack. To a room full of wooden sculpture, small and big, finished and unfinished. No wonder she wanted her tool so badly. The artwork was diverse and beautiful. He touched them, amazed at how well finished they were.

"Nene." He gasped. She had to be here somewhere. "Babe, where are you? Come out to me. Please."

His gaze caught a crafted woman and child. It was finely-made, polished even. It was the smoothest and most beautiful of all her work. He picked up the heavy craft, hadn't imagined it would weigh so. He could already see this going on the floor right in front of his 64"TV in his house in Lagos. It was the perfect size at about one foot high. How could someone like this exist? He had to have her. What could he say to bring her out of her hiding?

"Sweetheart, you are so talented. Why didn't you tell me about this?" He spoke to no one but guessed she would hear.

He walked to a wooden cupboard leaning against the wall of the gorge where the hole ended and opened it. There he found a few neatly folded clothing and personal items. Nothing worth anything. He closed it and returned to sit on the floor, surrounded by a wealth of Nene's talents. There was a stack of books on a small stool and he picked one.

"Great Expectations," he muttered.

He opened the first page and read off the name of a professor. One of her teachers in the college of education she told him she attended for one year.

Come back to school, Nene. You are my brightest student yet!

There was a name and a number to call. Seyi took the book aside. He would reach out to this person even though the date was five years back. Nene had to go back to school, and this gave him the idea. He packed all her books, about ten of them, and took them to his truck. Then he returned and took all the artwork, including her work-in-progress.

Alone in the empty shack, he felt drained. He wanted to hold her again, remembering the night they spent on her mat at the entrance of the shack. She hadn't said a word about what she had inside. Probably knew he would insist on spreading her news. Her words resonated with him. She deserved to be a great woman. If this girl had been given a chance, she probably would be in some foreign country on some scholarship. He carried the mat from outside inside and lay on it. The curfew had already started so he knew he couldn't leave. And he didn't want to, either. Wherever she disappeared to, she would meet him here when she returned.

But he couldn't sleep.

"Mrs. Dada conceived a wonderful idea and used me to execute it in Ilesa, after I returned the first time. I would go there, make money for her and come back... And I made a lot of money for her." Nene coughed.

Seyi closed his eyes in deep pain. He knew it. He had felt it from the beginning. She was compromised. A beautiful girl like her, and on the streets would eventually end up there. Could he ever respect her after this confession?

"Prostitution."

She shifted. "Begging."

"Begging?!"

He rolled on the mat, unable to get her voice out of his head. The things she shared with him. His mother had all but confirmed Kunle wasn't Chief Iwaneye's yet the man had agreed to raise the "bastard" child as his own. Was it even a good idea?

Seyi believed her. Why would she lie about such a thing? "Did Kunle know his father?"

"I don't know. He never talked about it. He guessed though. I think. He hated Chief and told me the feeling was mutual." Nene sighed. "I don't think it was a good idea to have him live with Chief when Mopelola lives elsewhere."

"Did you know them? Kunle's father? Mopelola's mother?"

"Everyone knows everyone. And Idowu Dada has made coffins for every family in this town, big and small."

Seyi sat up. Nene didn't answer the question. And neither did his mum. Where were these people? Did they still live in Ikoyi? It all came together. Nene didn't talk about her mother either, but he was sure her grandmother would have told her a lot. There are reasons for everything under the sun, and he would love to have these questions answered. Yet, what bothered him most was the life this little girl from the age of six was forced to live. She knew too much.

"Nene!" He stood. "Look, I know you are hiding somewhere," he said at the top of his voice. "I heard everything you said, and I am so sorry I didn't remember what you told me about the market." His voice seemed to echo but he didn't care. "Darling, I am sorry. And I will never take your words for granted again. I'm staying here all through the night with you. Let's spend it together like last time, honey. You said you had so much to say." He chuckled. "I feel powerful knowing people's secrets around here."

The sound of silence that followed made him kick the small stool out of frustration, but his shoe hit something like a knob. He pointed the torch at it. It first looked like a small stone. Seyi bent over it and realized it was the wooden handle of a box, buried in the floor. He pulled with all his strength and it came off; the top of it.

Seyi gasped. Inside a small carton-shaped wooden case was a pile of paper. He picked one up. "Prayer point."

He dropped down to his knees and brought out all the sheets. "They come with their prayer points? And throw stones at her by day? What kind of sick people are these?"

Nene took good stock. Some were in a beautiful cursive handwriting he soon realized was hers, though most were in different ones. Each one though had a date and the name of the requester, in Nene's handwriting. Seyi could not believe it. At least he saw none from his mother or Mrs. Dada. But he found some Nene wrote out as prayers for them.

"Chinenye Dada! Will you stop this nonsense hiding and come out here? I'm looking through your prayer points sheets. And I've taken all your books and artwork." He paused. "You're mine, all of you."

The wooden box also had journals, and recipes, and poems, so many poems. She wrote everything. She started writing after Kunle died and didn't seem like she was able to stop. A lot of what she told him was in her writing. There were names and addresses and phone numbers, email addresses. She didn't even have a cell phone or any device for that matter.

Why did she stay back in Ikoyi? She had contacts in Lagos, Ibadan, Ilesa, Akure, and many more cities in the South West. She could have lived in any of these places and had a seeming decent existence, but she stayed here.

Some of her poems were so touching and about other people.

"My mother." Seyi swallowed and devoured a poem on the woman Nene "talked" to every day.

There were several poems, some conversations with the woman who birthed her. He read about her most vulnerable days, her struggles. His eyes teared at some, and he cursed out at others. She was a scribe. For someone who told him Mrs. Dada stopped sending her to school at seven,

Nene's ability was pure genius. Seyi shut his eyes as her explanation came through in his mind.

"After the first baby came, Mrs. Dada asked me to stay home to help. They never sent me back to school. I peeped on my half-sisters' homework book, and eavesdropped on lesson teachers."

Seyi cringed. "That must be tough."

"I got by. Even did WAEC and JAMB. And passed. No funding anyway. So that dream died. Until–" She stopped talking.

He dusted something like sand off her nose. "Until?"

She exhaled. "I met a professor who thought I should go to school."

"You met him here? Do I know him?"

"I met him while in–Ilesa. At the Roundabout. Begging." She shook her head. "He gave me a thousand naira note! I forgot I was supposed to be deaf and dumb. I thanked him."

"Dangit!"

"Yes. He said he didn't think I was deaf and dumb. That he passed by the Roundabout every day and was keen on talking to me."

"Was he a young man?"

"Why would you ask?"

Seyi shrugged. "Maybe he was attracted to you."

"Maybe he was God-sent." She shifted a little, putting some space between them. "He got me into the College of Education. I would come to Ilesa, and he'd pick me to school, give me some money too so Mrs. Dada would never suspect. I did one year."

He moved to close the space between them. "Why did you stop?"

"Mr. Dada took ill. I was needed at home."

"She gave and gave and gave. Other people came first." He circled the room. "Nene, please now. You spent your whole life serving other people. Let me serve you. Let me spoil you. Let me–lemme–give you the life you deserve." He rested his back on the cupboard she kept her personal items.

"Baby, I love you," he whispered, afraid to admit it to himself.

Nene pushed the cupboard back, sure he was gone, and crawled out of the hole she created behind it. He would never have found her unless he tore down the shack, and that was what she proceeded to do.

Chapter 21

There was no point sitting in the hole calling her out.

Seyi was hungry and angry at himself. He needed to freshen up too and much as he hated to have to return to his parents' home after bidding them farewell, he went. He would return later and if she was anywhere in view, he was going to overpower her, knock her out if he had to, and carry her with him.

The utility car Asuka used was parked in front of the house, and he wondered what she was here for. On the other hand, it could be anyone in the production crew using it, especially when Seyi did not see any driver by the car. He decided to enter the house through the front. The visitors would be in the parlour, and he was right.

Asuka and Oyinbo, the light-skinned driver who drove with Nene to the market the day before, stood in the middle of the sitting room alone.

"Ah, Seyi! Your mum was about to follow us to make a police–"

He arched his eyebrows. "Give me a break, Asuka. What are you doing here?"

"Did you find her?"

"Yes."

Asuka sighed. "Oh, glory. I was so worried. Frank said to tell you we can resume today."

Seyi snickered. "When were we supposed to resume if not today?"

"You know your director." Asuka smiled. "Do we then pick Nene up on our way?"

"She hasn't agreed to come with us."

Carol walked in to hear his reply. "God is answering my prayers then."

"Asuka, I'll catch up with you later. You can tell Frank I'll come in today." He headed towards his room.

He heard his mother tell Asuka to talk to him, and "follow him, please," and moments after he entered his room, she walked in without knocking. He sat on his bed and covered his face.

Asuka sat beside him. "What happened?"

"She's not talking to me." He heaved. "The only way to bring her now is to force her."

"It was the most horrifying thing I have seen in my life. Do you know what she did to deserve that?"

Seyi covered his face. "They all ask for her help. She must have some powers, yet they despise her."

"Did she tell you about anyone she may have offended?"

Seyi stared at her for a second. "She has never spoken evil of anyone. Never–she told me only of what people are, do."

Asuka moaned. "Being outspoken can get you into a lot of trouble. I was called a snitch for doing it only once, and never forgiven throughout high school."

"Nene is outspoken when she decides to speak at all."

"I think she's a really sweet girl, though. You need to decide what you want to do with her. With Jenny in Lagos, you know."

"She's–different. I have nothing to think about–about Jenny." Seyi threw back his head. "I feel like a jerk."

Asuka squeezed his hand. "Nene, you met her when she came with the kids, right?"

"No, she didn't come with the kids." Seyi frowned. "I thought I told you–"

Asuka clasped her hands. "I know. I was just confused. She's the one that was your brother's friend."

"Yes." Seyi narrowed his eyes. "What are you thinking?"

"Nothing at the moment. Just that..." she shrugged. "Maybe she hasn't been forgiven all these years."

Seyi drove to the hidden tree an hour later after getting Asuka to leave. He had bought a big raffia bag from a store and arranged Nene's artwork inside. The papers he put in files according to what they were.

"If I don't return by evening, then I've gone to Osogbo," he told his parents. "I'll call to let you know."

The first thing he noticed was the way the crooked path down the gorge seemed to have been covered. It wasn't obvious to the normal eyes but now leaves had been cut to conceal it even more. Seyi removed them and knew at once what happened.

He gasped. "Nene, why?"

More branches filled the hole and this time, he had a problem locating the small passage, which was totally blocked. He pulled out rubble of stones and wood and leaves for several minutes before he cleared enough space to crawl through and when he got to the other side, he saw what he feared. The shack was gone, dismantled and the wood trashed. Whoever, Nene he suspected, did this either had a lot of time on their hands or had help. Nene had neither. He didn't imagine she would bring anyone here to assist her but he realized he knew little about the woman he now had a huge crush on. Suffice to say, he still feared to be in love with her.

He couldn't think of his feelings as anything less.

The shack area was so clustered he couldn't find space to stand, and he returned to his truck. She had sent him a strong message and his heart hurt just thinking about it. He drove around town for half an hour and returned to his parents' home. He wasn't in any right frame of mind to go to Osogbo not knowing where Nene was. Knowing she had destroyed his point of direct access to her.

He locked the door behind him and arranged her wood-work in places he thought were appropriate in his room. The mother and child he set on the floor beside his dresser, and it occurred to him all at once. They were too many to use in his home. She could have a shop and sell. And if she didn't want to own a shop, he knew of places in Lagos where her art could be displayed in exhibitions. The thought excited him beyond reason, and he packed them back into the bag. He needed to find her first. Besides his longing for her, they had so much to accomplish together. He took the file that contained her journal and searched for names and addresses. She had so many, and some were in Ikoyi. He would start looking for her from the people she seemed to have trusted so much as to document their location.

There was a soft knock on his door. He didn't want to see anyone. He wanted to go out and talk with people Nene knew. Beg them if need be to help him find her.

"Seyi?" Carol called. "Are you there?"

"Yes, Mum?"

"There's–you have a visitor."

He stood. "Who?"

When she did not say anything, he opened the door and scowled. "Who is it?"

Carol clasped her hands. "Please, I know I have offended you. I'm just asking you to forgive me."

"Is this why you said there is a visitor?"

"Don't be offended. I'm just–I only want to be a good mother to you. So much has happened."

"I've heard you. I am not offended. Now please can I have my privacy?"

She inhaled. "Someone is here to see you."

"Well, does the person not have a name?"

"You don't know her directly. Her name is Sade."

Seyi frowned. "Sade? From where?"

"She is–she is Nene's–Mrs. Dada's daughter. First daughter."

Seyi tsked. "What does she want to see me for?" He side-stepped her. "Don't bother."

He strolled to the sitting room, eager to send the girl away.

"My half-sisters let me read their books sometimes." Nene's voice echoed in his brain. "Sade would even tell me to say the alphabets after her."

Sade Dada must have changed her skin colour more than a couple times to have it in such a dark-green shade at horribly visible points. She was a copy of her mother though and had a lovely figure. All this Seyi noticed at one glance. She should be twenty according to Nene's age but with the heavy make-up and tight clothes she looked thirty or older.

She smiled, displaying a surprising set of beautiful teeth, and a gap. "Hello, Seyi." She purred.

He was almost double the silly girl's age. What did she want? He arched an eyebrow, caught off guard by her effrontery.

Sade giggled. "My mum said your crew had left but you'd be here a bit longer and could socialize."

He folded his arm across his chest. "She did?"

"Yes."

Her husky voice crept over the back of his neck.

"So, how will you like me to entertain you?"

For a moment, he just wanted to say the first vulgar thing that came to his mind. Instead, he folded his arms across his chest.

"Amuse me, Ms. Dada."

She bent forward. "That's an open invitation, Mr. Iwaneye."

Chapter 22

Adunola was one of those women who lacked the intelligence to take initiative on her own.

She sold cheap gold in the market, a trade she inherited from generations of the women in her family, mother, grandmother, great-grandmother and beyond. Seyi could well understand why she would stay in this business. She knew nothing else. After the embarrassing scene in his parents' parlour with his father walking in just at the right time to rescue him from the seductress Sade Dada, who must have thought to grope was cool, Seyi wanted to find Nene and leave the forsaken town as fast as he could.

The woman Seyi had heard so much about, and whose name and address was the first in Nene's journal had three little children all wearing nothing but underpants, their noses running despite the hot October weather. As he realized in the past week since the Olukoyi died, many people now knew his father would be king, and scrambled about to please him. Sometimes, he liked it.

"Kabiyesi l'ola." Adunola slurred. "Sit down." She shoved one of the munchkins of a child, Seyi still could not decide if they were boys or girls.

The greeting amused him but this was not the time, nor the person he wanted to get warm with. She actively participated in "stoning" Nene, and he needed to get to the bottom of their story.

He took the low wooden stool she offered. "Are they triplets?"

Adunola giggled. "Alakori's last gift before he died."

She didn't answer his question, but he let it pass. He was taken by her response. Did Nene know the man was dead?

"Alakori, is that your late husband's name?"

Seyi knew it was not.

Adunola made the giggling sound again, and Seyi soon realized it wasn't out of amusement but awe.

"I stopped calling him his name since he decided to be a near-do-good. An alakori."

"Oh, I see." Seyi sighed. "I heard he was sick, sorry about that."

"Who can we blame? A witch decided to suck his blood." She rolled her eyes. "You can't touch a witch, or she will suck your blood too."

Seyi frowned. "I thought Alakori had AIDS."

"Hian." Adunola snickered. "AIDS. A witch kills someone, what do you think doctors will call it? They must find a name for it. What is AIDS?"

"That's the problem, Adunola. Your husband was sleeping around with men and women alike–"

Some women walked by, paused at the entrance of Adunola's stall, and seeing she had a visitor, moved on.

She screeched. "It's not true! That witch Nene killed him."

Seyi arched his eyebrow. "Why would she kill him? What would she gain?"

Adunola coughed. "She is a witch."

"You don't really believe that, do you? How did you feel when they brought her to the market and beat her up?"

To Seyi's astonishment, Adunola covered her face and wept. He looked about and noticed they were all alone.

"I'm sorry to upset you," he mumbled.

She looked up, her face all wet, her nose dripping. "Alakori was a fool. Nene was my friend!" She whispered. "She always came to help me with the children and with my shop." She hiccupped. "They made me flog her with koboko. They told me she was the one who was sucking my husband's blood. They naked her and beat her. Heh-Nene!" She sniffed. "She was like Jesus. She forgave everybody and ran away from town."

Her timeline confused Seyi but he let it go. "Where did she go?"

"Nobody knows. After a month, she quietly came back."

Seyi frowned. Nene hadn't told him Adunola's husband was dead. "Did you speak with her?"

Adunola nodded. "Yes. But only in the night when nobody will see us. She didn't want anybody to see us together so they will not start treating me like a traitor."

Seyi clenched his fist, wanting to hit something. He lowered his voice to control his emotions. "Do you know where she is, please?"

"When she ran away the last time, she went to Ilesa."

Seyi jumped to his feet. "Thank you." He was going to find Nene in Ilesa if he had to turn the big town inside out. But first, he had two more stops.

Adunola jumped to her feet too. "Kabiyesi l'ola!" She hailed.

"Thank you. And please get treated. You and your children." He headed out. "For HIV."

Mopelola could be his twin. She had the same eyebrows, and the dimple in the chin only him and his father had. These besides the original shade of dark their milk chocolate colour was, and the same hairline. Seyi couldn't determine her height because she was seated, her new baby in her arms. The room looked spacious and clean. This woman must either have help from somewhere or be a superwoman. From what Nene told him, she was born a year before Kunle, which made her four years younger than him.

She smiled, giving off straight white teeth set on a dark gum. Seyi could swear his father's teeth looked like this when he was this age. Now they had a few missing, replaced with artificial ones. He had his mother's pink gum, perhaps the only feature he got from her.

"Please sit." Mopelola waved at a single chair he suspected was made by Nene giving designs carved in the sides.

The furnishing in the room was simple, and classy for what he had expected of his crippled single-mother sister. She breastfed her tiny baby from a rocking chair while her wheelchair was parked next to it.

"Nene told me you'll come."

Seyi paused halfway into sitting. "She was here?"

"This morning."

He lowered himself into the cushion of the chair. "She dismantled her–her room. Do you know where she is?"

"Not now." Mopelola stared at him. "She has told me so much about you." She chuckled. "Since you returned, she hasn't talked about anything else."

"You two are very close."

Mopelola sighed. "I'm one of the reasons the town hates her. She stood by my mother and me when no one else will."

"Where's your mum?"

"Hmm, she left after the pressure was too much."

Seyi scoffed. "She left you here?" He looked her over. "Like this?"

"She got married two years ago. I told her to go." Mopelola shrugged. "We've lived here all these years. She needed to be happy."

"Why didn't she take you and leave when the pressure, as you say, got so bad." He stood and paced. "I don't understand. Why do people stay here and–and suffer from the town?"

She smiled. "It may be easy for you to move wherever you please. Not everyone has the privilege."

He shoved his hand in his pocket. "Nene left several times and kept coming back. Which I don't understand. She could be living in Ibadan, teaching English to primary school children."

Mopelola laughed. "No wonder Nene likes you. Hmm. There is a lot more to leaving or staying." She sighed. "I know at some point I wanted to be here. To succeed here. To show my enemies they could not chase me away from my home."

"Such decisions a'times makes no sense.

"And I agree. Nene thought I was foolish as much as I thought she was." She smiled. "We are like children when we are together."

"She makes me feel like that too." He rubbed the back of his head. "I don't know why she's avoiding me now."

"To protect you."

She moved her sleeping baby off her breast and laid her on her shoulder. Seyi watched with awe, curious but unable to ask the questions at the tip of his tongue. Who was the father? How did she get pregnant? How did she cope alone? Nene would know and tell him but where was she?

He arched his eyebrow. "To protect me?"

"There are three women in this town. The three black pots." She counted off her fingers. "Mrs. Dada. Olori. And Yeye Loja, the head of the market women's association." She snickered. "They control everything in this town. They are not on the same team either. See them as the black witch, the red witch, and the white witch."

Seyi squinted. "In that order?"

"Yes."

"Mrs. Dada is the black witch. She's my mother's best friend and Nene's stepmother." He paused. "Furthermore, you are my mother's rival's daughter, and Nene is your best friend."

"You get the picture." The baby made a loud belching sound and she smiled. "Good girl." She continued to rock her in that posture. "The black witch and the white witch are always at par. The red witch switches sides as she pleases but they are all very powerful."

"And evil." Seyi closed his eyes. "Nene knew all of this, of course?"

He knew there were evil forces definitely but didn't think his nice little town was this dark. He paced thinking of his main motive of visiting Mopelola. To find Nene, but now he could understand why she would hide, and live in a hole, and hate going to the market. What he could not understand was why she didn't leave and go elsewhere.

"We all do. Ikoyi is a small town." She said it as though he should know by now.

And this made him let down his guard. He wanted to find Nene and take her out of here, but he needed to know everything. Obviously, she knew much more than she disclosed. Mopelola would have to fill him in.

"Okay, this town is small and evil, ruled by three evil women and everyone belongs in a camp–"

"Not everyone. Your Nene does not belong anywhere. She's the only one bold enough to openly denounce all of them."

"What camp do you belong?"

"How will you understand even if I tell you?"

It made no sense. The serene town of Ikoyi without the crazy traffic, simple people going about their businesses...

"Is that why you can't leave?" Seyi had never felt so frustrated. "Is that why Nene has refused to leave?" He grimaced. "Makes no sense to me. There are strangers in this town. You can't tell me everyone belongs to a camp. What about the churches and mosques?"

"I've told you how it is." She shrugged. "Nene told you why she can't leave, didn't she? People here need her. I need her. And I can't leave because I will not let anyone chase me out of my town." She leaned over the side of her rocking chair and pulled a cradle.

Seyi moved closer. "You need help?"

"Thank you." She handed the tiny baby to Seyi. "Please put her down. On her side."

She was too small, and Seyi thought he would drop her. Mopelola didn't even look over to be sure he did the right thing. Instead, she lifted herself to her feet first and then gripped the arm of the wheelchair and dropped into its seat. It looked practiced, like something she had done all her life. Seyi watched her, the baby clutched in his grip. He was yet to know the full story behind her disability. All he knew was that his mother nearly killed her mother during her pregnancy.

With Mopelola seated, he proceeded to lay the baby down. It was tougher than he expected and Seyi realized he was sweating when he returned to his seat. "She's so small."

"Hahaha, she is. She's only three days old."

Seyi gasped. "You must be very strong."

"Nene helped me deliver her here. I didn't have any complications. I thank God."

Seyi did a quick calculation. The night he didn't find her, she must have been with his sister. It annoyed and placated him at the same time.

"Does our father know you're here? Take responsibility?"

Mopelola nodded. "He pays for this place. Sends money for my upkeep."

"That's good." Seyi wanted to ask about her daughter's father. "So you mean Nene will not come with me to Lagos unless you agree to move too? You're the reason she's here?"

"Huh?" She burst into laughter. "You don't even know Nene at all. She's in this town for many people."

"How can I find her, please?"

"She'll find you. When she is ready."

Her words seemed final. She locked his gaze as though to tell him she was done. He stood, a cloak of defeat stifling him. He walked to the door and turned. He just couldn't leave like this. He didn't know where else to go, who else to talk with.

"When she comes to see you, please tell her I was here." He swallowed. "I need her too."

"I will tell her."

He took a deep breath. "Thank you, Mopelola." But he didn't leave. He stood at her door and stared at the floor. "You will soon be the princess if Daddy is installed king," he said. "I hope our father will do the right thing."

She laughed. Something he realized she did a lot and Nene did none of. He imagined how they were when together.

"You think I want to move to the palace with the black witch's best friend?"

She made a lot of sense.

"You're right."

"Thank you, but I'll jump and pass." She laughed more.

Her pleasant disposition made him relaxed. "Can I ask you something that has bothered me for some time?"

She rolled her wheels close to her baby and checked. "Yes?"

"Do you know Kunle's father?"

Mopelola stiffened and slowly lifted her head to glare at him. "Why do you want to know?"

Up until now, his sister had answered all his questions easily. This reaction got him interested more.

"I just wanted to know why my brother killed himself. It's obvious to me Nene was just the easy target to blame. And I didn't know he had a different father...it bothers me if he knew he had a different father." He rambled but couldn't help it. "Well, Nene told me everyone knows everyone, and I was wondering–" He shrugged. "No one seems to mention a name."

"Sit down, my brother. Let me tell you a long story."

Chapter 23

"**A**ll bastard looks like his father."

Nene looked nothing like her father. Besides the dark skin, of which Nene's was far superior, nothing. According to Mopelola though, Kunle was a splitting image of the vet doctor.

Idowu Dada laughed. "See my daughters."

His rhetoric was not lost on Seyi. The man must be the village moron everyone called him, married a witch, what else was there to expect? Six daughters, and if he counted Nene at all, that was seven. Seyi glared at Nene's father, disgust etched on the threads of his fabric. Armed with the information Mopelola gave him, he needed to see Idowu Dada. He didn't think it would make a difference to anything, but he at least felt he owed Nene that one confrontation. She would not agree to his plan or method, but he wasn't in any "camp" and didn't care if his mother was a witch or not. He could not be touched or harmed by any of their devices physical or spiritual. Just like Nene, he believed in the "most high," and though he was yet to let her know how deep his convictions were, he wanted to have this one opportunity.

The coffin maker was in his workshop, a small shed joined to his house facing the road, where he always was, sawing away. Two young apprentices worked with him, and he barked sputum-filled orders at them, countering himself several times.

Seyi snapped. "Nene only has a shade of your complexion."

"Huh, Nene. Her mother was yellow like mango." Idowu winked and bent backward, stealing a quick glance towards the main house. "We are banned from talking about Nene's mother, Adanne or her beautiful mother." He snickered. "Those two omo ibo just came to mesmerize all of us. Even in old age, the mother broke many homes." He chuckled.

"Why didn't you accept Nene?"

Idowu bent backward again and gasped then shook his head. "Omode o moogun! She'll be dead by now." He heaved a heavy sigh. "Adanne died. But this Nene," he lowered his voice. "Her head is strong."

Seyi wasn't impressed. "Why didn't you draw her closer to you? Even if you didn't want to publicly–?"

"Sshh! Aha, did someone send a curse to follow you here?" He pointed towards the road. "Get out of here, oloriburuku!"

Seyi was taken aback by his sudden aggression until he saw Mrs. Dada approach.

"Ahh, Prince Seyi! Wow, so good to see you. Sade is inside. You said you should first say hello to Daddy?" She laughed. "Come inside."

He should answer but it seemed his tongue was glued to the roof of his mouth. His heart thudded. There was an

immediate change in the atmosphere he could not understand.

Seyi knew the power of God when he opened the door of
his truck and got inside. He was sure his legs didn't carry
him out of there. Call it fear, or mind tricks, Mrs. Dada had
an evil presence beyond comprehension. Twice saved first
from the daughter and now a plate of porridge, he decided
all he just needed was to leave town. Nene would have to
come later, and he didn't know how. It broke his heart, but
what could he do? No one knew where she was. He didn't
think she could have gone to Ilesa or elsewhere. Mopelola
just had a baby, and she would want to hang around and
help. He could stalk his sister's house just to see her, but
Nene knew how to appear and disappear like an SSS agent.
The thought made him smile as he imagined her in such a
role. More important to him though, he wanted to hold her.
The yearning made his loins twist.

He pulled up in front of the house and knew something
was not right at once. In a few hours, the curfew would
start. He planned to leave town before it did, so he could
keep his job. Already he could imagine the rage going on
in Frank's head. There was no need to argue it anymore,
it was a mistake to come to Ikoyi to work. He should have
come on vacation. With all his clothes in Osogbo already,
he didn't even know why he came back here...a strong urge
to confront again. This time his father.

Seyi struggled with the decision to drive out before he
faced whatever stood waiting for him behind the closed
front door. He didn't seem to be in control anymore and this
confused him. No wonder he was never drawn to return all

those years. He pushed out of the truck. He could still drive to Osogbo, probably stop one more time at Nene's, see if she dared return to the mess she created. The yearning he had for her was intolerable. If he didn't find her, he didn't know what he would do. But if he did, he was going to carry her, gagging if necessary. She would never set foot in this town again if he had any say in the matter. The information he'd gathered made his head heavy and light all at the same time.

The smell of rice and stew accosted him, and his stomach rumbled. It was way past lunchtime and he hadn't so much as had a cup of water all day. Still angry with his mother, and now his father, he just wanted to go into his room, pick whatever he thought he needed, and leave. But he walked into the kitchen instead, following his stomach's leading and stood frozen. If it was Nene turning stew from his mother's pot on the fire, he would not have been more surprised.

"Jenny! What are you doing here?"

His fiancée laughed. "Surprise!"

Seyi's jaw dropped and his phone rang. To collect his thoughts, he picked the call without checking who it was.

Frank yelled. "Where the f...k are you?"

Seyi hung up on him. Jenny blew him a kiss. "Hello, handsome."

Chapter 24

A stream suddenly appeared, and she leaped in.

Seyi laughed. She beckoned to him and he shook his head. He couldn't swim. Some supreme force pushed him, and he was in the water with her, splashing away at each other like little children. He liked it, especially because she laughed so hard. The stream was shallow enough to wade through. They ran across and were back in her cave.

"Hide and seek." She screamed and ducked into a hole.

"Be my guest." He followed but didn't find her. "Ready or not, here I come!" He entered every hole. "Nene!" Panic gripped him. "Where are you?" His voice echoed.

"You win! Come out, I surrender." He seemed to go around and round, ending up inside her shack with all the wood artwork.

He panted. She couldn't disappear. "Nene!!!"

She jumped on him from behind and they both fell on the floor. He covered her face with kisses as she squirmed, laughing hysterically.

He growled. "Nene! Don't fight me." But she slid out of his hold. "Nene!"

Someone tapped him, and he startled awake.

"Seyi? I can't believe you came here."

He opened one eye, and then the other. There was sweat on his forehead and lips. "Hmm?"

Jenny mopped sweat from his face with her hand. "Why did you come here? We looked for you everywhere."

He sat up. The old couch in the store at the back of the house wasn't all that comfortable and he hadn't thought he would sleep off on it. His father's house wasn't so big and this storeroom had once been one of five bedrooms.

"I'm sorry. I came here to check out my old books."

Jenny grunted. "Old books? Hian, Seyi. This place is so stuffy. Let's leave here, please."

He followed her to the parlour where his parents waited, wondering why they let her roam the house. She had never been here. Who invited her? His mother most likely. This meant she had been snooping through his things and his phone. Right now though, he just wanted to be out of the town, take Nene with him if he could, and return to a normal life.

"You found him." Chief stood. "Now, I can go to bed."

Carol stood too. "You cannot go to bed. What is it? Are you not even concerned one bit about this family?"

Chief stopped in his tracks. "Which family?"

Seyi dropped into the couch. "What time is it?" He said as he checked his watch. It was just about 8pm. "I'm famished."

He stood and walked into the kitchen. As he dished out some rice and stew on to his plate, he heard his parents exchange harsh words. Instead of taking the food back to the parlour with him, he decided to eat in the kitchen. There was no doubt he came from the most dysfunctional family ever, and he never knew.

Jenny walked in. "They are really very angry."

He finished the food in his mouth and took a sip of water from his glass. "What are you doing here?"

"Your mum thought I needed to be here."

"In the middle of a work week?"

"I took days."

"Look, Jenny." He ate two more spoonfuls. "Just go back tomorrow morning. You should have called me before you headed out here." He tsked. "You don't even know my mother."

Jenny sighed. "She sounded desperate. Said I was the only one who could talk sense into you." She moved closer and pushed into his arms.

He set her aside. "No. You can't talk any sense into me, and you should have told her." He ate more food. "First thing in the morning, leave."

Jenny gasped. "See how you are talking. We are engaged to be married. Why should I not be able to talk sense into you?"

"Because you can't. Listen." He dropped his plate on the counter. "You should just go back to Lagos. I'm not having any conversations with you. I didn't invite you here." He picked up the food and continued eating.

"Seyi? Me?"

"Why am I even standing here." He dropped the plate and headed for the door.

She raised her voice. "Is it true a girl here is—you're having something to do with a girl here."

"My mother called you. Ask her."

He stomped out of the kitchen and would have headed to his room and locked himself in but he decided to finish all the business he had with his family before he went to lock himself into his room. Early in the morning, he would go and look for Nene and if he didn't find her, go to Osogbo. His heart hurt just thinking about it but there was no helping this issue now. He'd see Mopelola again and make her understand how desperate he was to get Nene. She was the woman of his dreams, and he had apologies to make for the way he had not believed her, the way he treated her.

Seyi knocked and entered his father's room. Chief Iwaneye lay on his bed, face up. "She's going to kill me one day with her nagging."

"You're going to be king, from what everyone is saying." Seyi sat on the edge of the bed. "She will want to be queen at least."

Chief shrugged. "She said you vowed not to come for the coronation."

Seyi shook his head. "I never said that."

"I know." He heaved a heavy sigh. "I'm just tired. With the politics already ongoing about this kingship, I want to come home to peace."

"When I'm gone I guess everything will come back to normal for you all." Seyi stared at his father. "I never should have come anyway."

Chief sat up. "I could have warned you. I'm sorry."

Seyi closed his eyes. His heart constricted at the thought of all the toxic information he's had to take in about his mother and now his father. There was no doubt in his mind, he needed to talk it over, get it off his chest.

"You knew Kunle was going to kill himself, Daddy." He inhaled through his mouth. "In fact, you drove him to it."

Chief Iwaneye was quiet and Seyi popped his eyes open to stare at him. "Won't you say anything?"

Chief folded his arms across his chest. "Maybe it's time to tell you everything."

"I know everything." Seyi snapped. "I know Mopelola. I know the vet doctor is Kunle's father. What else?" He paced. "The day before my brother killed himself, you told him the new vet doctor was his father. Only a few people knew until you spilled it out!"

"I was tired of seeing him, Seyi. Do you know what that was like? He was the spitting image of his father." Chief glared at him. "And the bastard had the gut to come back to town after all these years. For what?"

Seyi sneered. "So, you got satisfaction Kunle killed himself."

"I only told him to go and live with his father."

Chapter 25

Something terrible would happen, and she would be blamed, Nene knew.

"You are too hard on yourself. How many times will I tell you?" Adanne leaned on the other side of the tree.

Nene laid her head on what should be her chest but was the bark of the Iroko tree. "My sweet mother, what can I do? They will kill me the same way they killed you. Then I won't have him, will I?"

"Nobody can kill you."

"It's not the first time, and the last time it happened, I vowed I would not let it happen again."

The black truck drove up and Seyi got out of it. Because she knew enough about this environment after living in this part of town for over twenty years, Nene dove behind the tree where the effigy had been and crouched. It broke her heart to watch him on the other side of the road early in the morning, immediately after the curfew. She didn't know he would return here and was on her way to pick herbal leaves for Mopelola's baby's bath.

She had dismantled her home after he took all her life's possessions away. It was an act of anger and frustration, but she didn't regret it. She needed to lay low till he left. All the crew members were gone. He would too, soon. She planned to remain in hiding until he did, then she would go back and get her job with Pade. The waters will settle and find its level. Ikoyi had started to accept her, she knew. If Seyi had not come home at the time he did, she would have started going to the market again, almost. Nothing of import was happening anymore. The town had come to accept its many minor issues. Then Seyi returned with his eyes on her, and the bored witches got interested.

He got out of his truck and disappeared into the narrow path that led to her former accommodation. He soon emerged as she expected, surveying the area. His lips moved but she couldn't read them or hear what he said. He returned to his truck but didn't get in. Nene lifted herself off the ground enough to get a better view of him. This side of the road hosted only a few houses and though on level ground, she knew how to hide between the trees. At night, she stayed in Mopelola's one-room accommodation, to help with the baby, and have a roof over her head.

Seyi removed something from his pocket and Nene bent forward. She soon realized it was his phone. She had never owned one but for the first time wished she did. It would be her life's joy to send him a message and probably call to let him know she was okay and he needed to move on without her. Her heart pounded. He paced the sides of his truck and scanned the area while he spoke on the phone. He didn't seem happy with whoever was on the other side of the call. After a few minutes, he hung up and threw the phone into the passenger's side of the truck through the small window space wound down.

Nene squatted when she realized he stared more at the other side of the road where she hid. Had he seen her? She couldn't cope. If he saw her, she would not be able to resist him. She bit her lower lip to keep from crying. She wanted him so much. The night they spent together resonated through her being. This was the life she wanted, to love and be loved. If only things could be different. If only she wasn't born a bastard if her mother had not succumbed to the senseless courting of a man ruled by his wicked wife. Or any wife at that.

Adanne should have known Idowu Dada was married. Did it help her mother just moved to town and was being scorned by the market women? No. Nene pressed her lips together. She was doomed before she was born.

"Nene!!!"

She jumped, her heartbeat doubled at the unexpected shout of her name. She leaned closer to the huge tree and peeped. Seyi was back on the other side of his truck, his back to her. He must assume she hid inside the holes.

His voice was loud and broken. "Nene, please."

Her lips trembled without control. The tears she thought she could hold streamed down her cheeks. All she needed was to step out. Call him, and he would drive her to paradise, but she couldn't. Too much stood in between then and the life they could have together. And what if his mother prevailed over him eventually? Or he got tired of her. She could not afford to forget he was in a relationship. She may just be a passing distraction. She would be making the same mistake Adanne made. Though Adanne didn't know there was a wife in Idowu Dada's life.

A trailer drove by at top speed, whisking air in her direction. The disruption took her attention back to Seyi. He walked back to the edge of the road, and swiped tears off his eyes. His shoulders shook, and he leaned over the bonnet of the truck. Nene could not take it anymore. She straightened and stepped away from the tree. If it would kill her, then she'd rather die now. But Seyi bent all the way and leaned his head on his hand. Nene knew he still cried because of the way his shoulders moved.

"Seyi," she whispered. Her feet felt heavy, glued to the ground. "I'm sorry." Her tears slid onto her lips. She sniffed.

He lifted his head and cleaned his eyes. With shoulders slumped, he turned back toward the driver's side of the truck and entered. Her heart screamed for her to cross the road, expose all her vulnerability and follow love. Risk being taken advantage of, and be ready to face his mother's, and her step-mother's combined antagonism. Her head warned of the damage she would cause by being so "stupid." How her mother loved a man who had nothing in stock for her, and how that unreasonable love not only claimed her life but caused her daughter unbelievable suffering in the last twenty-one years. It all came together, and she watched him pull onto the road and drive off. If he'd looked up once, he would have seen her right there, by the road.

Nene screamed. "I will never love again." She swung around and ran through the trees and houses back to the empty life she knew.

Just a split of a second passed by. The moment he pulled back into the road, he saw her. It was not his imagination. Nene was there the second a car drove past. He made a neck-spinning U-turn, almost colliding with an on-coming car. He did not switch off the engine before jumping out of his truck and across the road. She was gone. Nene was there just a moment ago and a cloak of emptiness covered him.

Something told him he would never get her.

Seyi drove around the area for almost ten hours and finally hit the road to Osogbo to continue with the perfect life he lived before returning home after ten years.

Chapter 26

Seyi put the phone on speaker while he completed his remaining minutes on the treadmill.

"Find a hobo to do this, Frank. Not me." He rolled his eyes and listened to Frank for more than a minute, then he hung up without a reply.

Frank hated being hung up on and this meant Seyi would have to make-up, which meant Frank would make a request, which meant he'd not be able to reject...

"Crap."

He got off the treadmill. No need to call his director. He entered his bathroom and got a cold shower. Then pulled out a small suitcase. This was not going to be a long trip at all. He would give just one day.

Despite the million pleas from the palace, and from the king himself, Seyi checked into a hotel in the nearby town of Iwo along with his crew members though they didn't mind if he stayed with them or not.

"I'll see my father tonight," he told Frank once they checked into their hotel.

Frank grimaced. "Why do I have a strange feeling I'm going to be searching for you online. Again."

Seyi rolled his eyes. "Whatever. See you all at dinner."

"I just need you at the festival tomorrow. Looking on flick." Frank winked.

The Olukoyi's palace had been renovated nicely, with fresh white paint on the three buildings in the premises. A small green area was being cultivated around a freshly constructed walkway, and the driveway itself looked refurbished. Matched with other palaces he'd been to, this rated low but not in comparison to what the former king had. The two-story building the king lived in itself seemed bigger from the front and Seyi suspected his father added some structure to it.

Seyi's heart thudded in apprehension. Ikoyi remained his hometown but he hated it with passion. Everything he wanted got lost here. He had never stopped thinking about Nene, how she looked and smelled and tasted. No other woman drew him after all this time. His life revolved around his job and keeping fit. He couldn't even socialize as well as before. Driving through the Ikoyi square, seeing the Ikoyi Ben, gave him physical and emotional pain.

During the coronation of Chief Iwaneye as the King of Ikoyi, Seyi had purposely taken a trip to Ghana to cover an episode of his show on the slave trade. It gave him the excuse he needed to not return home. And a year later at his father's first anniversary, he bluntly told his parents he would not be at the ceremony. The revived Ikoyi Yam

Festival should pull him home, but it didn't. Without the blunder with Frank, who seemed particularly interested in this festival, he would be in his three-bedroom apartment in Lagos, nursing a wound that continued to fester. Several times the urge to drive through town looking for Nene rose from his belly but soon quenched at the realization that she did not want him. She'd stood beside the road and watched him on the last day, watch him cry over her, shout her name, and when he noticed her, she ran. He couldn't forgive or forget or deal with such a rejection.

A tall, muscled palace guard dressed in the attire made from the ancient deep blue "damask" fabrics but a modern design of trousers and a monkey jacket, something new to the palace as well, walked him through a hallway with beautiful artwork, to his father's private room. Seyi had never entered this room as a regular citizen. Though just a little bigger than a standard formal parlour, the designer did a good job with the arrangement of classy palatial chairs lined on either side of the throne. Three steps led to a beautiful gold rose carved throne chair in ivory damask fabric and gold buttons. Two smaller identical chairs flanked the king's.

Seyi moaned. "Daddy."

He imagined he would come and take one of those seats? And then it hit him. His father may have married a second wife.

Chief Iwaneye, the Olukoyi of Ikoyi entered from an exit behind the throne, dressed in a simple, long, white kaftan, cap and leather slippers. Seyi prostrated to his face in the customary way but his father pulled him up and hugged him.

"Thank you for coming." Olukoyi sat in one of the armchairs in the room and motioned Seyi to take another. "See, I prepared a seat for you by my throne. Praying you will come and take it."

Seyi laughed. "And here I thought it was meant for a second wife."

Olukoyi growled. "No way! I may not be a happily married man, but I won't make the mistake twice."

"How is Mum?"

"Busy. Today she's meeting with the women cooking for the festival tomorrow. Too busy, which makes me a man with plenty of time and peace."

"I know this is not the time or the place to talk but I do really appreciate the man you are. The father and husband you are." Seyi sighed. "I doubt I would continue to stay with a woman–"

"Ah, by-gone. Two things. I cheated first. And we never wanted to marry each other, our parents forced it." He clapped. "So, do you want me to show you to your room? I personally supervised the renovation."

Seyi chuckled. "I can't stay here. My crew is–"

Olukoyi stood. "Nonsense. I command you. As king."

"Daddy–"

"Ikoyi has only one prince. You. They want to see you tomorrow in your full glory." The king walked towards the exit he came from. "I should show you the whole palace. Your mother may be anything else, but she is a great queen! She manages this palace–" His voice faded.

Seyi reluctantly followed him.

Olukoyi opened a large room with a king-size bed and several pieces of furniture all in blue and grey highlights. The curtain and carpet matched, and three windows showed different views of the town square, the Ikoyi Ben, and the shopping mall. Seyi walked to one and for a moment saw Nene seated on the Ikoyi Ben, where he'd seen her reading her Bible. His heart raced.

"...and that witch, Mrs. Dada, may be anything but she supports your mother like no one else. Much as I hate her, she helps keep things going–"

"What is her first name? I've always wondered." Seyi kept his eyes glued on that spot, willing her to appear. If he stayed in this room, he would never stop staring at that view.

"Carol? Why would you wonder–?"

"No, Mrs. Dada. Everyone calls her Mrs. Dada. Doesn't she have a first name?"

Olukoyi laughed. "I never asked." He walked over. "I see you like this view. It's my favourite too. Though I don't get it this good in my room."

"It's a beautiful view."

"Let me tell you a story." Olukoyi winked. "I heard it was the former Olori's room. She wanted to keep it. Marry me." He guffawed. "Marry another witch? They want me to die before my time. Come."

Seyi smiled. Frank would almost have a fit if he didn't return but he wanted to sleep in this room and stroll down when it was too dark for anyone to care and sit on the same place Nene sat reading her Bible.

Nene paced the room in circles, singing and rocking on her feet every two steps she took. The moment she stopped, Funke wailed, and she continued.

Mopelola rolled in on her chair. "She has still not slept?"

Nene nodded. "Today is harder. But she will sleep."

"Maybe we should go outside. The air is cool."

"I was wondering where you went for so long." Nene shook her head. "Maybe I should not have made that ramp for you."

Mopelola laughed. "It slides like the highway and coming in is as easy as going out."

"So where did you go?"

"Market. I thought I should buy small food since it will be closed tomorrow."

"Mopelola!" Nene gasped. "You're not telling the truth. There's plenty of food in the house. Tell me."

Mopelola pouted. "Palace."

Nene exclaimed. "So far? What is happening there?"

"Everything. The prince arrived today. Everyone is talking about it. The king wants everybody at the palace tomorrow night after the yam festival. They want to do a big party where Prince Seyi will meet beautiful girls and choose a bride." Mopelola spun her wheelchair around. "It is so exciting."

Nene turned away. He was here. Back after almost two years. It would be easy to find a woman for him. Ikoyi girls had always been seen as the most beautiful in the region.

"That sounds interesting, Mopelola. No wonder Sade rushed here to ask me to come and make her hair for her tomorrow."

Chapter 27

Seyi had no way possible to work.

The Olukoyi called impromptu meetings with chiefs, discussing how to make Ikoyi a prime location in the area. They had tours of the palace and the town with several people who came in from different parts of town till late in the night. The king was like a baby having his first taste of juice.

"All the sons and daughters of Ikoyi, home and abroad, are going to be here!" The king clapped. "This is going to be the grandest Ikoyi Yam Festival ever, and it will keep getting better." He turned to the man who took over his chieftaincy title, Otun. "Do you know we have Cable TV this time. People from all over Africa. And Seyi brought his crew too. They have reach all the way to the Caribbean Islands."

Seyi woke up early the following morning and finally took a long walk at the square. Not a word from Nene in almost two years. He had thought he would die from wanting her but he's still alive, barely getting by but alive. No love in his life anymore. He couldn't even look at a woman. He returned to the palace and had a long warm shower. Olukoyi must have spent millions of naira on the palace. The bathroom had all new fixtures. At some time in the night, the king must have gotten his men to bring his stuff because he found his suitcase in the walk-in wardrobe.

"You can live here now, Prince Seyi. You will be my personal assistant. We have world organizations interested in our small town. What that boy who came from London tried to do...we can do it together."

His father said so many impossible things. But living in Ikoyi was the most preposterous. With all the drama the last time, falling in love with Nene and losing her all in one week, he could not stay here. He dreaded having to return. Every day he woke up and polished her artwork. He had a room for her in his house where he romanced her. The two pictures of her he had slept on his bed with him. He'd take that life over any other a million times over. Definitely, not what his father planned – a party to showcase women for him to choose from. Totally absurd.

"Once we find a beautiful girl in Ikoyi for you, all your worries will be over."

"I won't be at the party, Kabiyesi!"

That was the most preposterous!

Sade looked so beautiful, as Nene had never seen her before. Even Mrs. Dada grabbed her by the neck and hugged her. The first of such an expression of appreciation.

"No girl in this town will beat you in this competition," Mrs. Dada said. "The queen has told me he will not return to Lagos. You see how beautiful the palace is now, that is where we will live."

Sade snickered. "You will not follow me to live in the palace with my husband."

"Why not? Don't I deserve to start enjoying after all these years? Will I be the coffin maker's wife forever?"

Sade kissed her teeth. "He will go out of business if you leave him. Or who will be killing people for him?"

Nene slid out of the house. Three other girls wanted her to make their hair and it was getting late. With the late announcement of the party, many young ladies who made no special arrangements scrambled around. All shops were closed, and the two hairdressers charged exorbitantly, taking undue advantage. Sade had relaxed her hair and planned to wear it with some waves, but braiding made her face pop.

The parade was almost over when Nene entered Mopelola's house.

"Ah, you're back!" Mopelola rolled toward the door. "I've been waiting since."

Nene dropped into the chair. "The parade is so colourful. Thank God for Kabiyesi Iwaneye who has brought celebration back to town." She looked around. "Where's Funke?"

"My mother came from Osogbo. Funke is with her."

"Hmm. That's good. Is she not seeing her for the first time?"

"She is."

Nene opened the pot of okro soup she cooked the day before. "I'm famished."

"They didn't give you money or food?"

"I know how I make my money." Nene took a modest portion and licked it. "Hmm. So good." She found two wraps of fufu in the small food warmer and took one." Did they ask about Funke's father?"

"They didn't this time. She looks like her father now." Mopelola rolled her eyes. "I don't care. I love my baby."

"You have nothing to worry about. At least Funke makes you happy." Nene sat back and ate. "I want to go and watch the events at the palace. Should we go together?"

"Heh! Yes. And you can dress up for it too." Mopelola wheeled across the room. "We need to get ready."

Nene froze. "Dress up. For what? In what?"

Mopelola continued to the wardrobe in her room. "I lied yesterday, Nene. I didn't go to the palace. I went to the market." She opened the wardrobe and removed a bag. "Adunola brought it for me while you were away."

"Adunola?" Nene dropped her bowl of food on the floor. "What are you talking about?"

Mopelola opened the bag. Nene leaned forward unsure what to expect.

"Look, we all know how much the prince loves you. He looked for you everywhere. Came to all of us, even Adunola. He went to Mrs. Dada's house to ask after you."

Nene's mouth dropped open. "What?"

"I thought I was being your friend by forcing you to come and live here, and not tell you all of this. I thought you will be able to live a normal life but nothing has changed." Mopelola removed a long-beaded dress from the bag. "When we heard the prince was in town, we went to borrow this from the new bridal shop."

Nene gasped. "You don't even know my size." Tears sprang to her eyes. "I don't even know my size." She rushed to the improvised kitchenette, washed her hands and returned to Mopelola's side. "It's so beautiful."

Nene lifted the dress afraid it would disappear. "Huh, it pricked!"

Mopelola burst into laughter. Nene wished she could join her.

The yemoja traditional dancers finished their interesting rollercoaster dance and Kabiyesi Oba Adekunsiwa Adeyemi Iwaneye, the Olukoyi of Ikoyi rose in his purple royal robes and beaded crown. He proceeded to announce and appreciate all the celebrities and philanthropies, sponsors, friends of Ikoyi, sons, and daughters home and away. Then he introduced his vision for the party, and how he hoped the only Prince of Ikoyi will find a wife.

"Tonight!" He shouted, and everyone screamed. "Let the competition begin!"

Seyi rolled his eyes for the umpteenth time. He didn't know what he was doing here. His head, and feet ached from all the walking and dancing through the town at the yam festival parade. His father had him seated on one seat from the throne room, his mother on the other, flanking the king. The square had been turned to a massive carnival ground with seats all over the place, between buildings, stalls, and the Ikoyi Ben. Whoever set the place up had a good vision and knew how to manage space. With the throne room emptied and set on the square, adequate space had been created for presenters and dancers. It would also serve as the runway for the most beautiful girls in Ikoyi who stood the chance to become the Princess of Ikoyi. The mere thought had Seyi roll his eyes again. Asuka stood across the grounds with the cameraman and waved at him, her face beaming.

"Enjoy it, Seyi! This is your chance to find love." Her voice rang in his mind.

"I found love," he'd snapped.

The program presenter took over and announced the girls in twos. They walked out, danced, spoke, marketed themselves. Some were awkward and silly, some strikingly beautiful, some had poor fashion. None struck him in any particular way. He noticed Sade Dada, Nene's disgusting half-sister. To cap up their vanity, her mother escorted her. Seyi endured the longest of the spectacle cringing every other minute. He wasn't the only one who felt choked, and the presenter walked over and had them removed so the last two girls could be presented.

Then all twenty girls in the pageant came forward and Davido's Aye blasted from the loudspeakers.

Olukoyi leaned over. "Prince Seyi, go and dance with the woman of your choice."

Seyi wanted to protest but his father straightened and turned his attention back to the floor, nodding his head in rhythm to the music. Sade Dada danced forward, beckoning on Seyi with an outrageously seductive move. This was more than he could bear. Again, he questioned how he could have allowed himself to be pushed this far.

He stood, and the crowd went wild with excitement. The presenter spoke into his microphone.

"Let's make welcome Prince Seyi as he takes the dance floor."

Seyi didn't know he could be so nervous. He beckoned on the presenter and whispered in his ears. "I want all the bachelors in Ikoyi to join me on the dance floor."

The guy chuckled. "I will make the announcement after you get there."

Seyi mentally rolled his eyes. "Okay. Thanks."

He straightened, pasted a smile on his face, and walked confidently forward. He would dance with Sade Dada. She was the prettiest of the bunch anyway.

Chapter 28

Nene bowed her head. "Mopelola, are you sure. They will throw stones at me."

Mopelola smiled. "They won't know it's you."

Nene gasped. "Is that supposed to be assuring. What if someone knows."

"It's a compliment, my dear. Go now. He's going to dance. Go!" Mopelola let go of her hand and pushed her forward.

They had been sandwiched in between two shops for almost an hour while Nene contemplated the best time to show up. She knew these grounds like the lines on her palm but didn't imagine it would be so decorated. She and Mopelola waited in the southern part of the shopping mall. Right behind was the end of the street and several trees and some shrub. Nene had chosen this location in case things went sour. It was a quick escape route and with the set-up, no guests sat around the place. No one would harm Mopelola. She was the king's daughter though she continued to reject her father's offer to bring her to the palace.

Nene swallowed. "He looks so happy."

"That is a fake smile. Can't you see how miserable he looked throughout the competition?" Mopelola pushed again. "Go." She hissed. "See, he's going to dance with your sister."

Nene stared at Seyi as he took the steps down the throne toward the dance floor. He looked so handsome in a white damask voile embroidered mid-length slim-fitted shirt and matching trousers. He wore white leather slippers and a cap he removed and gave to a nearby guard exposing hair cut close to his scalp. She closed her eyes. She couldn't look. The voice in her head asked her to turn and run. But she did this before and lived the most miserable of days and nights. Her heart urged her to risk this. You'll never find love if you don't seek it out.

She dragged in a calming breath. "Wish me luck."

"You have it. And my blessing. And the blessing of Adunola, Sade, Temitope, Idowu Dada, the owner of the new bridal shop, my mother, your late mother and grandmother, Prince Seyi–"

"I get it." She stepped out into the open.

When Seyi took Sade's hand, Queen Carol stood and clapped. Mrs. Dada rushed forward to stand beside the queen and Seyi rolled his eyes before he could stop himself. Nowhere on earth would he marry this girl. She was too young for him, not half as pretty as his dream woman and too closely related. He focused only a moment on her though before other men flooded the dance floor.

"I knew I will win." Sade turned and pressed a tad too close. "I mean, who else?"

"The one who didn't show up." But Seyi only smirked.

With other men on the floor, he hoped to disappear. Take complete leave and return to his room to nurse his pain.

"Aaa-yeee! Aaaa-ye." Sade sang with a voice so off Seyi cringed and she pressed toward him. "She no wan Ferrari–"

A noise came from the end of the floor with murmurings. Davido continued to blast his love song but no one seemed to dance to it anymore. A path parted and it seemed directed toward Seyi and Sade. Though people danced all around them soon they were alone on the floor with a woman no one seemed to recognize.

Seyi glared down from ivory stiletto heels, beautifully-shaped burgundy painted toes to smooth long legs. Up to a white knee-length dress with a detailed arrangement of small coral beads. The small-sleeved gown skimmed her body exposing accurate female curves like none he'd ever seen. She half-smiled and batted long eyelashes. Her lips were the same burgundy shade of her toenails. No foundation could make a face so soft or so tempting for a touch. This was natural.

The one who would replace the one had arrived.

Seyi stole a glance in the direction of the throne, his throat closed. Olukoyi stood with all the chiefs and he stepped toward the new girl. She pressed her lips together the way he knew only one other person ever did. Realization hit him in his groin before they got to his eyes.

He could not let anyone know and she nodded. She was the one.

Seyi let out a long victorious laugh and grabbed her hand. "Nene," he whispered into the hollow of her neck. She giggled. The sweetest music to his ears.

"This is unacceptable!" Sade stomped away.

Murmurs of "Who is she?" "Who knows her?" filled the arena.

Nene whispered back. "Let's get out of here."

"I don't have a car. I didn't come with–I rode with the crew." He pulled her into his arms as the DJ started playing Tosin Martin's Oloomi. "Let's dance."

Nothing mattered around them. Nene giggled. "I can't dance on high heels."

"Your legs are so beautiful. Were they always this long?"

"Only my legs?" She gasped. "All you see are my legs."

"Your hair." He dug his hand in the braided locks. "I like the braids. So long. You never–this is all your hair?"

From the corner of his eyes, he noticed the dance floor had filled again but Mrs. Dada and his mother were headed towards them with a tearful Sade in tow.

He growled. "Let's get out of here."

"I know where." She pulled him through and people parted way for them.

Like two little children, they ran to the end of the mall and entered a small alley where Mopelola remained in her wheelchair. Nene ran to her and hugged her neck.

Mopelola screeched. "I was right."

Seyi laughed. "Thank you. Whatever it was you did."

Mopelola's eyes widened. "They followed you."

Seyi and Nene turned and saw his mother with Mrs. Dada and Sade, and several people headed in the direction of the alley.

Mopelola spun her wheelchair to form a small barricade. "Run! You know where."

Nene grabbed his hand and followed the corners she had used for many years to escape the assault. Had they recognized her too? Seemed so. But she wasn't going to let anyone win her ever again. The only person who could stand between her and love was Seyi himself. But this man laughing and running with her through trees and shrubs, across the road and beyond, didn't seem likely to stop her. They came to a stop, panting under a huge mango tree with no fruits and underneath was clean and grassy.

Seyi pulled her to him and fell on his back with her, laughing hard. All the trail was gone, and a full moon provided necessary illumination. His mouth clashed with hers before she could roll off or protest. They ate at each other hungry enough to hurt.

"I will never let you go. Never again."

I'm not going. I've learned my lesson–"

He cut her with a deep kiss. "I miss you. I thought I'd die." He continued to kiss her.

She came up for air, hysterical with joy. "I was just so afraid. I ran like I always did."

He cupped her face. "For your information, I hit the gym and the stadium when I returned to Lagos. You run again, I will catch you. I can beat the world's fastest man right now."

She sat up. "Catch me now." She took off.

He growled. "What?"

She could hear him behind her, but she increased her speed. One of the heels came off and she took the other off, so she could run faster. The trees hindered some of the moonlight, but she knew her way around, and then it struck her. She couldn't hear him. She stopped running and laughing. Had she lost him again? She breathed hard unable to think it.

"Seyi?" She called, and he jumped out from behind a tree causing her to scream. She fell into his arms. "You scared me."

"You can never escape me again." He leaned back and produced the one foot of her shoe. "This gave you away."

"Hmm. I can't live another day without you, Seyi." She looked into his eyes. "I love you."

He groaned and covered her lips with his. "Where are we?" He took out his phone. "I want to call Frank to pick us up."

She gave him the landmark. "Where are we going?"

"The Palace."

He made a call and spent the wait time bathing her with affection. They rolled on the bare ground, staining both their white attires with leaf and mud.

The palace buzzed with activity when they arrived, and Nene felt a familiar foreboding. In the back seat of the saloon car, Frank and Asuka came to pick them with, she leaned her head on Seyi's chest as Frank drove in and searched for good parking with Asuka's help.

"Is my make-up all gone?" She raised her head. "People will now know it's me."

"I didn't notice you wore make-up. And anything any-one does to you, they do to me." He kissed her forehead. "Don't worry your sweet head."

Asuka turned to them. "Do you want us to wait for you?"

Seyi looked at Nene. "For her. She'll feel better."

Nene sighed. "They can leave if they have to." Then winked. "You know I can run."

Seyi dropped his gaze to her lips with the same hunger she'd seen in his eyes so many times. "You'll be fine." He dropped a peck on her lips.

The night was far gone and close to midnight already. Seyi held Nene's hand and walked into his father's throne room with Frank and Asuka in tow. The set designers were arranging the chairs and the throne.

"My parents may have turned in," Seyi told the rest. "I think you can–"

"We didn't turn in, Prince Seyi." Olukoyi walked in from behind the throne. "We all waited for you to return."

Queen Carol walked in after him followed by Mrs. Dada, and her six daughters, the youngest a fifteen-year-old who looked nothing like her mother or Idowu Dada. Many of the young women filled the room from other parts of the palace. It seemed someone had blown an alarm. Seyi tightened his hold on her, and she pressed her lips together, waiting for the worst.

Olukoyi climbed his throne but did not sit. "I personally wanted to meet the beautiful woman who stole your heart."

Seyi frowned and turned sharply to Nene. "They still can't recognize you," he murmured.

Nene nodded. "Seems so."

Seyi took a step forward with her. Sade leaned on her mother's shoulder, weeping while Carol clasped her hands tight.

"This is Nene, the woman of my dreams."

The room exploded with flashes of light. Cameras from phones blinded her but Nene held her ground and her peace. She wanted to cover her face or run as she always did. Seyi's warm hand gripping her cold one gave her reassurance. He was still here and that was all that mattered.

"No!" Queen Carol shouted. "Haba, Kabiyesi. Will you be looking at her like this?" She burst into tears. "She caused our son to die, please don't let this second one die too."

"Shut up, Queen Carol," Olukoyi snarled. "Come forward, Nene. Let me see you. You look so beautiful."

Queen Carol whined as another drama started with the Dada girls. Sade wailed aloud, and her sisters pushed at one another.

"He's mine."

"He's mine."

"Stop it!"

"He's mine."

The youngest laughed. "You are all joking. All joking."

Olukoyi waved at his palace guards. "Guards, remove these mad people from my palace."

The two guards stopped in their advance.

Olukoyi flew to his feet. "I banish you, Mrs. Dada from this town. If anyone sees you after tonight, let them throw stones at you."

"You dare not, Kabiyesi." She unwrapped a small gourd from within her wrapper and stretched it towards the king, muttering viciously.

Seyi and Nene raised their voices in unison in prayer. The room divided to those praying and those cowering behind Mrs. Dada. After several seconds, Mrs. Dada screamed and ran out of the palace squealing gibberish, her six daughters with her.

Queen Carol shouted. "I'm going with! I'm going with her." She ran after the Dada women.

Seyi swung around. "Mum, come back."

"Let her go, Prince Seyi. We need fresh air in this town." Kabiyesi raised his hands and clapped. "Let the celebrations continue."

A loud shout rent the air. Loud music blasted from speakers meant for the outdoors. And towners took to the limited space dancing. Nene noticed the servers from the square were inside with their food coolers and cold drinks.

Frank stepped up. "We leave in the morning. Are you coming or staying to assume your princely throne for a few more days?"

Seyi smiled at Nene and they both nodded. "We will stay for a few more days."

Frank shook hands with both and Asuka hugged. "So glad you found each other," she said.

Olukoyi beckoned on them. "I will retire now but enjoy yourselves. The party continues till dawn."

Nene wanted to go to sleep but the glimmer she saw in Seyi's eyes energized her.

He pulled her closer. "Come and dance, Princess Nene Adeseyitan Iwaneye."

They moved in slow rhythm to Lara George's A new day, oblivious to who noticed them, though half of the time all they just did was smooch.

Epilogue

Seyi hung up the call with his father and walked through the two-bedroom house he just bought in the high-brow Ikoyi part of Lagos. The irony of buying a house of his dreams on the same street as the name of his hometown was not lost on anyone. The last time his father tried to make him move back home he told him,

"I married a girl from Ikoyi, and now I live in Ikoyi, what more do you want?"

Nene dozed off with their new-born son on her chest on the balcony attached to the master bedroom of the one-story house. Seyi stared at them for a minute, his chest thudding with pride. He lived the life he imagined with Nene. She was the best thing that could ever have happened to him. He had news for her now though and much as he regretted disturbing her peace, he had to speak with her. Olukoyi wanted a quick response.

He woke her the way he enjoyed the most, placing a kiss on her lips. She opened her eyes and smiled.

"Hmm? Did I sleep off?"

"No." They both beamed.

He drew the single chair he took when they were both on the balcony closer and she sat up careful not to wake their son, Prince Adeniyi.

"Something wrong?"

"Mum wants to come back to the palace." Seyi sighed. "Kabiyesi refuses."

Nene frowned. "Why?"

"Well, his reason was that he didn't want her anymore."

Nene shook her head. "You need to prevail on him. We can't repay evil for evil."

"I know, darling. Kabiyesi didn't tell me the truth all along. Till now." Seyi smoothed a stray strand from her forehead. "He wants you to forgive her."

"Me? I have. I mean, there is nothing to forgive."

"No, Nene. There is everything to forgive. The whole of Ikoyi town punished you because of my mother and her friend." Seyi shook his head. "I still don't understand how you managed. But that is not the case anymore."

Nene swallowed hard. "I can't go back, sweetheart. I have nightmares."

"Nightmares?" He cupped her face. "You never told me."

Tears sprang to her eyes. "I'm terrified."

Seyi pulled her into his arms with their baby. "Mrs. Dada is no longer a threat to anyone. Her magic backfired and all she does now is drool. She can't harm you anymore. And my Mum is sorry."

"I just wonder why? Why did they treat me like that?" Nene sobbed. The little prince stirred. "Sshh," she cooed.

"You need a hug yourself," Seyi said.

He led her to put the baby down and covered her face with kisses.

"I do."

Seyi picked his wife and swung with her. "Let me see if I can convince you to return to Ikoyi with me."

He dropped her on their king-size bed and drowned her worries the best way he knew.

The End.

Acknowledgments

My late father, Dr. E. A. Ifaturoti, a mining expert and number one member of the Nigerian Mining and Geosciences Society. Also, I want to thank my mother, Mrs. Agnes Ifaturoti, who chipped in important notes. Thanks to Pastor Jesse Agede, who helped to compile the facts at some stage.

ARE YOU SAVED?

All that is written in this book may not be of much use to you if you haven't yet given your life to Christ. We cannot take difficult decisions unless we have the Righteous and Wise One that is greater than the devil to help and choose for us. The Bible says that "greater is he that is in you, than he that is in the world." (1 John 4:4 King James Version) And "we wrestle not against flesh and blood, but against principalities, against powers, against the rulers of the darkness of this world, against spiritual wickedness in high places." (Ephesians 6:12).

This is why I want to encourage you to take this important decision if you haven't yet given your life to Christ. I took this decision twenty years ago, and I haven't regretted it even for one day. Please pray this prayer of faith if you are willing to surrender your life to God:

Lord Jesus, I honour you. I praise you, and I acknowledge you that you are Lord. I know I am a sinner, and I ask that you forgive me all my sins. I want you to be my lord and personal saviour. Wash me clean and give me grace to serve you wholly from now on. Come into my heart to reign supreme. In Jesus' name, I pray. Amen.

PRAISE GOD, YOU ARE BORN AGAIN.

Now that you have prayed this prayer of faith, I admonish you to

•   Get a Bible and read it every day. (Start from the first four books of the New Testament to familiarize yourself more with your new commander in chief, Jesus Christ.)

•   Pray every day.

•   Attend a Living Church.

•   Introduce yourself to the pastor and seek further teaching. (You can join the foundation class and activity group in church. You are, hence, making yourself available to work for God.)

•   Tell others about your salvation.

May God help you in Jesus' name? Amen.

The Nigerian Child: My Vision

Then the LORD answered me and said: "Write the vision and make it plain on tablets, that he may run who reads it." —Hab. 2:2

More than before, it's time for the well-to-do to cater for the less privileged. Over the past few years, the Lord has laid this burden for The Nigerian Child on my heart, and I believe it's time to spread the vision. I have a desire to help and to instigate help for The Nigerian Child. There are currently five areas of help I have been able to identify.

1.   The Market-school Project: This vision is aimed at eradicating street and market hawking in the long run. The strategy is to erect schools in marketplaces where children hawking can take a few hours out to learn and then go back to their jobs. It is a long-term project and a highly capital intensive one.

2.   The Bread and Milk Project: Bread and milk will be given in the morning to children trekking to school just before school resumes. It can be done once a month, once a week, or every day or as rampantly as the provision is

available. It is not very capital intensive, and as little as N50 or $0.35 (US dollars) can feed a child with bread and warm milk.

3.   The Umbrella Project: This will help alleviate the suffering of children who hawk on the streets (while we work toward eradicating hawking on our streets) by providing umbrellas, especially during the rainy season. The umbrellas can also be useful during the scorching hot weathers. Umbrellas of different sizes will be given depending on the size of the child. Prices of umbrellas range from N350.00 to N500.00 or $2.50 to $3.50 (US dollars).

4.   The Sort-a-child Project: This is aimed at helping at least a child in whatever capacity you can. It can be by paying a sick child's hospital bills, buying food and clothing for a child, or paying a child's school fees. It can be as long as a lifetime commitment or a onetime affair.

5.   The Student Care Project: This is for secondary and tertiary students who can't afford their school fees. The idea is to help through the bob-a-job initiative.

The Nigerian Child vision is not another nongovernmental, money-spinning organisation. It is service to God and provision for The Nigerian Child. It can be done privately or corporately. The important thing is to help a Nigerian child.

I beg to challenge every church in Nigeria to adopt the sort-a-child project or as the Lord lay it on our hearts.

HELP!

Signed

- THE NIGERIAN CHILD

Also By Sinmisola Ogúnyinka

Blue Dawn
Frail Flesh
Scent of Water
Her Lover
I Loved a Slave
The Truth, The Lie and The Dare
The Days after that Night
Under a Red Delta Sun
Money Woman
I'll Tell My Story

www.ingramcontent.com/pod-product-compliance
Lightning Source LLC
Chambersburg PA
CBHW030936210726
48290CB00007B/2211